Sun Signs

Sun Signs

Shelley Hrdlitschka

ORCA BOOK PUBLISHERS

National Library of Canada Cataloguing in Publication Data

Hrdlitschka, Shelley, 1956-
Sun signs / Shelley Hrdlitschka.

ISBN 1-55143-388-5 (bound).--ISBN 1-55143-338-9 (pbk.)

I. Title.

PS8565.R44S95 2005   jC813'.54   C2005-900094-5

First Published in the United States: 2005
Library of Congress Control Number: 2004118008

Summary: While taking online courses, fifteen-year-old Kaleigh
learns that on the Internet, people are often not who they seem.

Orca Book Publishers gratefully acknowledges the support for its
publishing programs provided by the following agencies: the Government of
Canada through the Book Publishing Industry Development Program (BPIDP),
the Canada Council for the Arts, and the British Columbia Arts Council.

Cover Design and interior typesetting: Lynn O'Rourke
Cover font: (Astro Font)

In Canada:	In the United States:
ORCA BOOK PUBLISHERS	ORCA BOOK PUBLISHERS
BOX 5626 STN. B	PO Box 468
VICTORIA, BC CANADA	CUSTER, WA USA
v8R 6s4	98240-0468

09 08 07 06 05 • 6 5 4 3 2 1

Printed and bound in Canada

For Kyla, my favorite Aries
—S.H.

Acknowledgments
Thanks to Kim Denman, Diane Tullson
and Beryl Young for their ongoing encouragement.

Distant Learning Inc.
Term #2
Science 10 Research Project
January 9 – April 2

Assignment: Choose a science topic **Of Interest To You** and gather information on it. Using the Scientific Method (see attachment #1), form a hypothesis and conduct an experiment to test/support your hypothesis.

This assignment is in lieu of the traditional science fair project. Although this is the same kind of endeavor, as you are correspondence students, you will only be marked on the written portion of the project.

I will expect six progress reports over the next twelve weeks, as well as an initial proposal, and a final report due April 2. Also, before you go to too much work on your initial proposal, e-mail me with your topic and I will give you the go-ahead if I think it's suitable.

This assignment will be in addition to your weekly assignments, but will account for 50% of your final grade.

Have fun!

Mr. J. Selenski

Scientific Method
Seven Steps to Discovery

1. State a Problem

2. Gather Information

3. Form a Hypothesis

4. Experiment

5. Record and Analyze Data

6. State a Conclusion

7. Share Your Discoveries

State a Problem

Forecast For the Week of
Jan. 15 – Jan. 21
by B.A. Stargazer

♊

Gemini (May 22 – June 21)

Gemini, you can no longer ignore the project that's been left undone. A slight shift in your reaction to things is all that's required.

From: cosmicgirl
To: distantstudybuddies
Subject: calling all science 10 victims

Who else thinks science projects should be outlawed?? Have any of you started It yet? He says 2 choose a topic we're interested in. Yeah right. What if we're just NOT INTERESTED IN SCIENCE? Hey, Mr. Selenski? Did you ever think of that??? It's a mandatory course! We're not taking it because we WANT 2.

And get this. My horoscope this week is right on, as usual. It says I can't continue to ignore the project that's been left undone. Can you believe it? It's like it's directed exclusively at me. Do all geminis have science projects they haven't started yet? I don't think so. Okay, it can be argued that the word "project" could be interpreted in different ways. But still, you can't convince me there's no truth to this stuff. Take this week's cancer forecast. (Are any of you cancers? UGLY word.) "Your mood is totally upbeat. Your boss loves you for being innovative and a team leader." That is so NOT me. I don't even have a boss.

My horoscope also says I should shift my reaction to things. Fine. I'll just pretend that science is really cool. That I just can't wait 2 do a research assignment. That there are so many INTERESTING things I can study…

Not.
Science sucks.
Help!

Kaleigh

Hey Kaleigh, how about a project to determine which lipstick has the most stick? U could choose 5 different brands, apply them, then kiss your favourite guy for, say … 5 minutes apiece. The one (lipstick — not guy) that's still on at the end wins — assuming u still care after 5 minutes of kissing!!

You're right. It's a bit lame. Okay … how abou … which zit cream works the best? Yes? Mind u, it would be hard to find a control group. I can hear u now. "Okay zits. You, over here, the cluster on the chin—you're the control group and u only get air and water. Now, u, the cluster on the forehead, you get product A … and u —over here, around the nose … product B.

No? You're right. U probably don't even have zits. That's the trouble with this distantstudybuddies connection — we have no idea what each other looks like! Okay, how about … which tampon is the most absorbent? All us girls have to deal with that!

Okay, I've got it. You could investigate which love potion (the ones they sell at those sex shops) is the hottest. Or which tastes the best. Do u think Mr. S. will go for that? I bet he's pretty hot! :) (Has anyone ever met him? Is he for real???)

Just doing my best to help a distantstudybuddy in need.

Shari

From: 2good4u
To: cosmicgirl
Subject: Re: calling all science 10 victims

Kaleigh? R u blind?? U ARE SO interested in science already!
Do your report on astrology. i can't believe i have to point that
out 2 u.

2good

From: cosmicgirl
To: 2good4u
Subject: Re: calling all science 10 victims

Is astrology really a science?

Kaleigh

From: 2good4u
To: cosmicgirl
Subject: Re: calling all science 10 victims

Of course it is. Anything with "ology" at the end has 2 b
science.

2good

From: cosmicgirl
To: 2good4u
Subject: Re: calling all science 10 victims

You're right! How could I not see that?? It's a COSMIC science, 2 PERFECT for me! I could do research on how horoscopes are created ... but what about an experiment? Somehow I'd have to prove that astrology makes sense. That by studying the planets and stuff, astrologers can forecast the kind of day/week/year u are going to have. That the forecasts are accurate ...

I know! I'll get some of our distantstudybuddies to help me. They can keep track of how accurate their forecasts are ...

All of a sudden I'm excited about this. Go figure!

But first, Mr. Selenski.

Thanks, 2good! You're a lifesaver!

Kaleigh

From: 2good4u
To: cosmicgirl
Subject: Re: calling all science 10 victims

They don't call me 2good for nothing.
U r welcome.
2good

From: cosmicgirl
To: jselenski
Subject: Science Research Assignment

Dear Mr. Selenski,

For my Science Research Assignment, I would like to study astrology. I will write a report on how astrology works, and I'll set up an experiment proving that horoscopes are not just light entertainment.

Yours in science,

Kaleigh Wyse

From: jselenski
To: cosmicgirl
Subject: Re: Science Research Assignment

Dear Kaleigh,

Although this topic may be amusing, I don't take the study of astrology seriously, nor do I think you should. Kindly choose another topic.

Mr. J. Selenski

From: cosmicgirl
To: jselenski
Subject: Re: Science Research Assignment

Dear Mr. Selenski,

According to my dictionary, astrology is "the study of the movements and the relative positions of celestial bodies (that's planets and stuff, in case you didn't know) interpreted as an influence on human affairs. It assembles random bits of the universe in which you live into a pattern that makes sense." Mr. Selenski, astrology is studied by millions of people and has been for thousands of years and in lots of different cultures! For this reason, I hope you will reconsider and let me study it for my term research paper. Please!

Thanks in advance!

Kaleigh Wyse

From: jselenski
To: cosmicgirl
Subject: Re: Science Research Assignment

Dear Kaleigh,

Although you haven't convinced me that studying astrology is a worthwhile pursuit, you have convinced me that you are interested in it. Therefore, I will allow you to study it this term. Be sure to follow the Scientific Method, as outlined in the attachment you received with your assignment. I admit, I am curious about what on earth (no pun intended) your hypothesis will be and how you will run an experiment. That said, perhaps you can turn this skeptical old teacher into a believer.

Good luck.

Mr. J. Selenski
P.S. I know what celestial bodies are, thank you very much.

From: cosmicgirl
To: distantstudybuddies
Subject: calling all leos!

Hey everyone! Mr. S. is letting me do a report on astrology for my science research project. Cool, huh? A big thanks to 2good for the idea!

Here's the thing. I have to do an experiment, and I need some of u to be my guinea pigs. I've decided to study the astrological sign of Leo because they are the party animals of the cosmos and sound like fun! If you are a lion (born between july 24th and august 23rd) and want 2 help me out, all you'd have to do is read a daily, weekly, monthly and maybe even yearly astrological forecast (supplied by me) and record how accurate it is. You'd have to send me weekly reports on your findings, written in YOUR BEST English (in case I have to submit the data).

So, who wants to play?

Kaleigh

From: 2good4u
To: cosmicgirl
Subject: Re: calling all leos!

Kaleigh, has selenski really given u the green light on this topic? He must be getting soft in his old age. i was actually kidding about the whole thing. Anyway, u r not going 2 believe it but i'm a lion, and i'm in if u want me, though i don't know about that best english shit. R u serious?

2good

From: starlight
To: cosmicgirl
Subject: Re: calling all leos!

Hey Kaleigh, can you believe it? I'm a leo and i love stargazing! Count me in.

Shari

From: blondeshavemorefun
To: cosmicgirl
Subject: Re: calling all leos!

cosmicgirl,
i'm a leo and i'm all yours.

blondie

From: cosmicgirl
To: distantstudybuddies
Subject: Re: calling all leos!

U guys Rock! And u must all luv science! In less than 1 hour I have 3 leo subjects and at least 6 others who want me to change the astrological sign I'm studying to a different one so they can play. I wish I could include u all, I really do, but I'm thinking there'd be way too much data to handle. Who'd have guessed there'd be so much interest in astrology? Not Mr. Selenski, that's for sure.

Thanks thanks thanks!!! i luv u all!

Kaleigh

From: cosmicgirl
To: 2good4u
Cc: starlight; blondeshavemorefun
Subject: Leo team

It's official. You are IN!!

A few introductions are in order.

First, we have 2good4u, commonly known as 2good.

Then we have starlight, alias Shari.

Last, but not least, there's blondeshavemorefun (blondie).

Say hello. Shake hands. Maybe even a polite little cyber hug would be appropriate, for you are now the LEO TEAM. Is that RAD or what? Maybe my finished project will be so amazing, so mind altering, so so so … okay, so startling, that some scientific journal will pay me for it, publish it, and u (and i) will become famous.

Just imagine.

Cuz that's the only way something like that would ever happen!!!

Seriously, thanks to each of u leos for volunteering to be guinea pigs (my all-time favorite little rodent). I'll be in touch again soon.

May today's planetary positions bring you all heaps of positive energy!

With her head in the stars,

Kaleigh

From: blondeshavemorefun
To: cosmicgirl
Cc: 2good4u; starlight
Subject: Re: Leo team

hi hi. shake shake. hug hug.

blondie

From: 2good4u
To: cosmicgirl
Cc: blondeshavemorefun; starlight

party on fellow leos!

2good

From: starlight
To: cosmicgirl
Cc: 2good4u; blondeshavemorefun

i'm partying, 2good! hugs and shakes back to you, blondie.

Shari

From: cosmicgirl
To: jselenski
Subject: SCIENCE RESEARCH PROJECT PROPOSAL

Topic: Astrology

Problem: By studying the position and movement of the celestial bodies, can astrologers accurately predict events?

Method: I will use the library and the internet to research the history of astrology, how it works and the ways in which astrologers determine horoscopes using the cosmos. Then, using three

Leo subjects, I will gather data indicating whether the forecasts (previously supplied to them) are coming true. I predict that the results will demonstrate that the forecasts are accurate. This is based on my own personal experience.

Yours in science,

Kaleigh Wyse

P.S. Do you happen to be a Leo?

From: jselenski
To: cosmicgirl
Subject: RE: SCIENCE RESEARCH PROJECT PROPOSAL

Dear Kaleigh,

This is a very sketchy proposal at best, but I am glad to see you have addressed the first step in the Scientific Method, and that is, stating a problem. My concern with your project is that so many variables could impact your research and data collection, making the results questionable. For example, one variable could be the attitude of your subjects towards astrology. If they are firm believers in the "science"—like you—might this affect the results? Could this not potentially skew their data collection? Then there's the reverse. If your subjects are skeptics—like me—this too could affect the way they collect data. Just something to think about.

In the meantime, you may proceed with your research and data collection. And no, I am not a Leo. Guess again.

Mr. J. Selenski

P.S. I received a note from your mother indicating that you will be receiving radiation treatment soon. I am willing to give you an extension on this project if need be.

js

From: cosmicgirl
To: 2good4u
Cc: starlight; blondeshavemorefun
Subject: just checking

Dear (loyal) Subjects, (I feel like Royalty)
Do you believe in astrology (horoscopes and all that) or are you what Mr. Selenski calls a skeptic (non-believer)?

Kaleigh

Please start using "proper" spelling and punctuation in our letters re astrology. I am now officially collecting data.
Thanks.

From: 2good4u
To: cosmicgirl
Subject: Re: just checking

I believe in you, cosmicgirl, and if you're a child of the stars, so am I.

2good

From: starlight
To: cosmicgirl
Subject: Re: just checking

Hey Kaleigh. I'm a total believer. What's not to believe?

Shari

From: blondeshavemorefun
To: cosmicgirl
Subject: Re: just checking

I believe in Truth. (How's that for good English?)

Truthfully yours,

blondie

From: cosmicgirl
To: jelenski
Subject: One less variable

Dear Mr. Selenski,

Just thought you'd like to know that all my subjects are believers (I think—although I don't really understand the response from the one who calls herself (himself?) blondie. What's her/his real name, anyway?).

Sincerely,

Kaleigh Wyse

P.S. I don't need an extension, thanks anyway.

P.P.S. Are you an Aquarius, whose traits include intelligence and honesty as well as unpredictability and contrariness? (No disrespect intended!)

From: jelenski
To: cosmicgirl
Subject: Re: One less variable

 Nope, not an aquarius either!
js

Jan. 21

Dear Immortal Gemini Twin,

The cosmos is unfolding as it should, the last week hasn't been bad, and us mortal Geminis are counting our blessings.

Right.

Let's see. What were those blessings? Hmmm.
1. *I'm alive.*
2. *I'm not dead.*
3. *I can still count.*

I did start the science project, just like my weekly 'scope said to. It might be okay. My Leo team seems cool. More than cool, really. Maybe life can be fun again. For a while, anyway.

I can hope and have faith. After all, I am a Gemini. And we know what that means.

That's it for this week,

Your mortal (for now) twin sister

Gather Information

Forecast For the Week of
Jan. 22 – Jan. 28
by B.A. Stargazer

♊

Gemini (May 22 – June 21)

You may feel you've entered limbo land this week, Gemini. Waiting is the worst. Get active. Build an interesting life outside of the main event.

```
------------------------------
```
From: 2good4u
To: cosmicgirl
Subject: hey girl!

how goes the research on astrology? i'm dying 2 get started as a guinea pig. i've even practiced up on my pig squeals. 2 bad u can't hear them.

and i was wondering, are you a fellow leo, one of the chosen ones?

2good

ps. did you know guinea pigs eat their own poop?

```
------------------------------
```
From: cosmicgirl
To: 2good4u
Subject: Re: hey girl!

It's not going well AT ALL! There's all this stuff I had no idea about!! Ascendants. Transits. Rectification. Progressions. Aspects. Nodes. Who would have guessed? It's all complete mumbojumbo. I never thought astology could be so complicated.

Here's an example. There's a "transit" that is currently taking place. I quote: "Saturn will be making a passage through Cancer from June 4 (this year) to July 15 (in 2 years! Talk about a slow passage!). Though we may complain about what we don't have under the influence of Saturn, we will learn some valuable lessons from it. Saturn also sits right on the ruling planet—the moon—for the next year. This will bring many changes. Our political rulers will change. We will have to make sacrifices." Blah, blah, blah. Like, who cares!!

What have you gotten me into, 2good?! (And how can u get me out?!) How do I write a report about something that makes absolutely no sense! AHHHHH!!!!!

Kaleigh

P.S. Are you telling me YOU eat your own poop (because u are my guinea pig)?
P.P.S. No, I'm not a Leo. I'm a Gemini—flexible, logical, quick-witted and mentally ambitious.

From: 2good4u
To: cosmicgirl
Subject: Re: hey girl!

if you're so logical and mentally ambitious, how come you're having so much trouble with this science report? why don't you go straight to the source and ask the horse—i mean an astrologer—for help?

and what can you tell me about leos—other than we are party animals—which i already know?

2good

From: cosmicgirl
To: 2good4u
Subject: Re: hey girl!

u are SO smart, 2good! i can't believe i didn't think of that myself, especially as i'm so ingenious (another gemini attribute).

The horoscopes that i like to read are written by someone named b.a. stargazer. i checked, and her email address is listed on her webpage! i'll email her right away. She's unbelievable, as i'm sure you'll find out when i get to the experiment part of this project. Her forecasts are always so accurate, and she's right on when it comes to geminis. She says we have a lightness of spirit and a faith that a happier world is a possibility.

yep.

She says geminis are kind, considerate and creative. We are also lively, versatile and communicative.

uh huh.

Gemini is the sign of the twins. One twin is mortal and the other dwells with the gods. (I'm in weekly communication with my immortal twin! lol)

She also says we're talkative. moi? never! :) Okay, just the mortal one.

Anyhow, once again u are a lifesaver, and not the kind that comes in 100 flavors. (i wonder if being a lifesaver is a leo trait?) Other leo traits include being ambitious, a lover of the limelight, extroverted, confident, exuberant, dramatic and charismatic. Do you see yourself in that description? i suspect you're confident, (and maybe just a little overconfident?) judging by the name you've given yourself in your e-address!

i hope all the planets are lined up in perfect harmony for you today. kaleigh

----

From: cosmicgirl
To: B.A. Stargazer
Subject: Science Report

Dear Ms. Stargazer,

I think you are an amazing astrologer. Everything you say about my sign is true of me—the good stuff, anyway—and your weekly horoscopes are brilliant. Thanks to you, I'm even thinking of becoming an astrologer someday.

I am a distant learner, which means I don't attend school but do all my work through correspondence. Right now I'm writing a report on astrology for my science class. At first my teacher didn't want me to choose this subject because he doesn't think astrology is really a science. I am out to prove him wrong!

I have 3 distant-learning buddies who are Leos and who are going to track whether your predictions come true for them. I already know your predictions are always dead on for me. It should be fun! I also have to Gather Information on astrology (my science teacher is big on the Scientific Method). I'm wondering if you could help me with my report. If so, my first question to you is, how exactly do you determine what is going to happen for each of the signs on any given day, month or year?

Your loyal Gemini,

Kaleigh Wyse

From: cosmicgirl
To: 2good4u
Cc: starlight; blondeshavemorefun
Subject: Data collection

Hey Leos. Good news for me! I found my favorite astrologer's website and on it are our daily, weekly, monthly and even yearly horoscopes. This saves me from having to cut and paste and send them to each of you.

Check it out at www.sunsigns.com

Even though I haven't done all my Information Gathering yet, you might as well get started with your data collection. Here is what I suggest you do:

1. Right now (okay, after you're finished reading this) print out the monthly and year-long horoscope for the sign of Leo. Memorize them. (just kidding!)

2. Print out the Leo weekly horoscope on the Sunday of each week.

3. Check out the daily horoscope each morning.

4. After you put your jammies on each night, spend a few minutes thinking about your day and decide whether the daily horoscope was accurate. Then reflect on whether the weekly one is coming true. The monthly? The yearly?

5. Keep an online journal with your reflections and thoughts that you can attach to an email and send to me upon request. (Don't you just love my teacher-speak?)

Any questions?

Okay, ready, set, go!!!!!

Kaleigh—the bossy one

From blondeshavemorefun
To: cosmicgirl
Subject: just one question

what if one of your loyal subjects doesn't wear pj's?

blondie

From: cosmicgirl
To: blondeshavemorefun
Subject: Re: just one question

R U SERIOUS? No cuddly warm flannels? I live in mine!
Never mind, reflecting in the nude is perfectly acceptable.

Your Highness

PS. I used to think you were a girl. I know they say blonde girls
have more fun. Is it true about guys?

Kaleigh

From: blondeshavemorefun
To: cosmicgirl
Subject: Re: just one question

what makes u think i'm a guy?
blondie

From: cosmicgirl
To: blondeshavemorefun
Subject: Re: just one question

I don't know. Maybe because you sleep in the nude. That seems
like a guy thing. So what are u?
k.

From: blondeshavemorefun
To: cosmicgirl
Subject: Re: just one question

that's for me to know and you to figure out!

blondie

From: cosmicgirl
To: blondeshavemorefun
Subject: Re: just one question

Forget it! That will drive me craaazzzyyyy!

k.

From: blondeshavemorefun
To: cosmicgirl
Subject: Re: just one question

crazy is good! LOL

From: cosmicgirl
To: B.A. Stargazer
Subject: Science Report

Hi Ms. Stargazer,

Remember me? I'm the student doing a report on astrology. Even though you haven't had a chance to reply to my last letter, I felt like writing to you again. I hope you don't mind. I realize now that the question I asked you about writing horoscopes for each sign was unfair. It's so complex! You would have to write a whole book to explain that to me, wouldn't you? Lol.

I've been doing some more reading, and I think I finally understand what birth or natal charts are. I'm also beginning to understand that it is by reading the transits that the astrologer figures out how the cosmic energy affects us. Unfortunately, there are still LOTS of things I don't understand. You must have studied astrology for years and years before you became an astrologer! Is there a School of Astrology that you have to attend?

I always read your horoscopes. This month you mentioned that Uranus is moving into Pisces for the first time in eight decades and that Uranus is "seldom lucky, but always interesting." You said there would be "unpredictability overall." You also said that this would affect Gemini by shaking up our inner worlds. This does not sound like a good thing!

I have to admit, this forecast has me a little worried. I have had some seriously bad luck in the past year—healthwise—and my life has been anything but predictable. Can you tell me anything more about what this forecast could mean for me?

Your loyal Gemini,

Kaleigh Wyse

From: cosmicgirl
To: 2good4u
Subject: Let's get started!

Any time now, my furry little guinea pig, you can get started on the experiment. Are you still squealing?

By the way, do you know if blondeshavemorefun (blondie) is a girl or a guy?

Kaleigh

And what is YOUR real name? Rumplestiltskin?

From: 2good4u
To: cosmicgirl
Subject: Re: Let's get started!

no, i'm not rumplewhatshisname, but you've made an interesting observation. mr. rumple solved the fair maiden's problem in the fairytale, right? didn't he turn straw into gold or something?

so it would follow that since i solved YOUR problem (a topic for the science project), u need to guess my name correctly or you'll have to turn your first-born child over to me, as decreed in the fairytale. :)

Maybe blondie is a eunuch.

2good

From: starlight
To: cosmicgirl
Subject: Collecting Data

Kaleigh,

Have I got news!

But first I must tell you, this data collecting is too much fun. (I'm using my best English here, girlfriend, but seeing as I don't actually go to school, please excuse me if I screw up occasionally. LOL.) Anyhow, I've printed off the yearly, monthly and this week's Leo horoscopes. Wooeee! I can't believe I never thought of following this horoscope stuff more closely before. This Stargazer babe is cool. It's too soon to tell whether everything is going to come true in the long term, but after reading what she said about the coming year and this month of January, I sure hope so! My love life will be hot hot hot. LOL. As if that could happen here! (Although after what happened yesterday, you never know. But I'm getting to that.)

For this week, she said, "People notice you more than usual now and you're in fine form." Well, seeing as I live on a remote little island with only a handful of neighbors and almost no other kids, I thought that was totally not about to happen and maybe she wasn't so smart after all.

But (and you're not going to believe this, Kaleigh), just after lunch yesterday, I was sitting at my kitchen table looking out at the ocean, wishing I was just about anywhere else and wondering how on earth I was going to get noticed. Out of nowhere a yacht pulls up to our dock and out piles a whole family—a dad, a mom and two guys—aged 15 & 17! I thought I must be dreaming. I blinked my eyes a couple dozen times and shook my head hard, but when I looked again they were still here! LOL! Apparently this family is taking a year or two off from their regular lives to cruise the west coast, but they were having some engine trouble so pulled up to the first dock they spotted. Both sets of parents tinkered on the engine most of the afternoon, so I was left with the guys, Matt and Chris. They are home-schooled, which is quite different—I found out—from taking correspondence classes like us. The biggest difference is that their dad is their main teacher. Can you imagine?

Anyway, I can't decide who I like better, Matt or Chris. They are both cute, super nice, smart and definitely not shy. They seemed about as happy to meet a girl roughly their age as I was to meet them! We spent the afternoon comparing notes about our various "schools," played computer games and hiked across the island. By the time the yacht was fixed it was getting dark, so they stayed for dinner and slept here (on their boat). After breakfast they sailed away (sob), but I have their e-addresses so we are going to stay in touch.

Kaleigh, it was the most fun I've had in weeks! It made me all that much more determined to get off this stupid little island and get a real life complete with boys, movies, sports, parties, music lessons, friends, more boys—you know—all the stuff most kids have every day.

Anyhow, that is my first report for your science project. Now I'm wondering how you're planning to tabulate this information. However you decide to do it, give Ms. Stargazer a big ✳ from me this week!

Shari

From: cosmicgirl
To: starlight
Subject: Re: Collecting Data

Wow, Shari, that was a good day. But I can't help thinking that it was all the eye-blinking/head-shaking that got you noticed. LOL

So that's why you're a distant learner—you live on an island. I can see how you might not like it, being so removed from everything, but believe me, there are definite advantages. For example, imagine going to school with a couple of thousand other kids and having to watch which hall you walked down because each one is owned by a different gang. Walk down the hall of a gang that doesn't like your particular color (skin or hair)/religion/sex/grade/sexual orientation/mother/father/brother/sister/astrological sign :) and you're in big big trouble. I should know. I've been to that school. And sports are not so great either. If you're not one of the best on the team, forget it. Coaches play the best players and everyone else warms the benches, if they haven't already been cut. I tried dance classes for a while, but all those hours in front of mirrors ... yuck. And besides, I'm not into looking like a toothpick, which is the right dancer look.

What else do you think you're missing? Parties? Oh yeah. Well, there's not as many of them as you'd think. Maybe certain crowds party more than others. Music lessons. I had them, but practicing every day can get a bit annoying. Boys, on the other hand ... Sounds like you met a couple of good ones yesterday. Can't wait to hear how your e-relationships go with them. I've heard some e-relationships get pretty steamy!

So why do you live on an island anyway? Let me guess. You're marooned and no one has ever found you? No, I guess that family from yesterday would have rescued you if you wanted rescuing. How about ... one of your parents is a prison escapee and has to hide for the rest of his/her life. No? Are your parents hippies with a grow op on the island? Hmm. I'm making myself— as Alice in Wonderland would say—curiouser and curiouser. A mystery.

Speaking of mysteries, do you happen to know 2good's real name, and whether blondie is a guy or a girl? And what's his/her real name?

My science report has actually become fun — go figure! I emailed Ms. B.A. Stargazer (the astrologer) with some questions. I told her I was thinking of becoming an astrologer myself—which isn't quite true — but I thought she might like to hear that. (Shh! Don't tell!)

Anyway, can't wait to get data from you again soon. Your English is very "good." LOL. Keep up the good work.

Kaleigh

From: starlight
To: cosmicgirl
Subject: Re: Collecting Data

Hi Kaleigh,

The truth is—I am a prisoner on this island and it sucks, big time. Let me explain.

My father is a marine biologist and is studying ocean currents and the migration of jellyfish. These studies take YEARS to complete. It is dead boring. My mom is a so-called "successful artist" and has a studio at the side of the house where she goes to paint, sculpt and do all that other good stuff. I didn't mind being here when I was little because I didn't know what I was missing, but NOW I KNOW! There is a ferry that comes to the island a couple of times each day and brings us the odd visitor and our mail. It would even take me to and from school on the mainland, but my parents are very happy to keep me isolated from the real world. What they don't understand is that I am TRAPPED and will ESCAPE at the first chance. They say I don't know how lucky I am to live in such a safe environment. Yeah right. It's a good thing I've got my books—they let me order as many as I want, and it's the highlight of my life when a shipment arrives. It's an even bigger good thing that there is email and chatlines so I know what is happening OUT THERE. I will never do this to my own kids!!

So now you know why I am a distant learner. What is your excuse?

Shari

P.S. Sorry, but I don't know anything about 2good and blondie except that they're Leos.

From: cosmicgirl
To: B.A. Stargazer
Subject: Science Report

Dear Ms. Stargazer,

I hope it's okay that I keep writing to you. I know you must be way too busy studying the stars and writing all those horoscopes to answer email from a person like me, but I like writing letters and will keep sharing stuff about my science project if you don't mind.

I finally got the first bit of data from one of my Leo subjects. She was very excited because her horoscope came true that day. I think she, too, is going to become a big fan of you and your horoscopes.

There's one thing that really puzzles me about astrology. I've noticed that almost all astrologers agree on the personality traits that describe people in each of the signs. But what they don't agree on is horoscopes. They are often contradictory— two astrologers forecasting completely different things. Aren't both astrologers reading the same set of stars and planets? I better get busy and find out why this is, because I just know my teacher is going to ask me about it.

Your loyal Gemini,

Kaleigh Wyse

From: cosmicgirl
To: jselenski
Subject: Progress Report #1

Dear Mr. Selenski,

It has been two weeks since you first gave us this assignment, so I decided it was time to turn in my first progress report. (See? Even if I don't do so great in science, I AM competent at math!)

As you may recall, I am studying astrology so that I can understand the formation of horoscopes better, and to figure out why they always seem to come true, for me anyway. (I suspect it may be a different matter for you!) So far I have selected three Leo subjects who are reading the same horoscopes (daily, weekly, monthly, yearly) to determine whether the forecasts match what is actually happening in their lives.

I have contacted the astrologer whose forecasts we are using. She hasn't responded yet, but I hope she will.

I have collected some data from one of my subjects, and it clearly showed that the Leo forecast for that week had come true for her. These early results are very exciting!

I'm having a little more trouble with the Gathering Information portion of the project. Astrology is way more complicated than I imagined. (I'm sure you'd be shocked, Mr. Selenski, seeing as you don't even believe in this stuff.) There are all kinds of words and terms and other stuff that I just don't understand. For example, have you ever heard of a Saturn opposition? Or how about a Jupiter transit? It's all very mysterious, but I'm doing my best to decipher the information so I can write a proper report. I will keep plodding away, but I expect the Record and Analyze Data portion of my report will be way more interesting than the Information portion. (Just thought I'd warn you.)

Anyhow, I hope this is enough information for my first progress report. Thanks for assigning this project. I'm having a lot of fun with it, and I am getting to know a couple of the distantstudybuddies better. It's also a great way to keep my mind off—you know—other stuff.

Yours in Science,

Kaleigh Wyse

P.S. So if you're not an Aquarius (and I was so sure about that!) you must be a Scorpio: resourceful, a researcher, as well as intense and strong-willed.

Jan. 28

Dear Immortal Gemini Twin,

Doesn't Ms. Stargazer realize how hard it is to "build a life" when you're stuck at home all day? Like I'm going to choose to go outside looking like this. The way people stare and then quickly turn away makes me crazy. I don't know what I'd rather they did, I just know I can't take it anymore.

The "main event" reference in the 'scope was pretty obvious. But anyone who's gone through this knows that it's impossible to get away from it. It's always there, a little vise squeezing your heart all day long. Just when you get your mind off it, bingo! You remember again and the squeezing is a little tighter than it was before. But she's right about the waiting part being the worst. It is. Waiting and worrying.

I miss my friends! :(What have I done? But Shari called me girlfriend. That's a start.

Thank God for email, and schoolwork.

Hey! Those Leo guys sound so cute. Can you give me a sign, O Immortal One? If they really are as cute as they sound … make the lights flicker.

I'm waiting.

Still waiting.

Are you sure? They SOUND cute.

Okay, maybe you and I just have different tastes in guys. Your idea of a hot one is probably someone in a white gown, with a harp and a halo.

And anyway, even if they are cute, they'd never look at me. Well, actually, they would look (stare), but of course then they'd look away real fast ... in pity ...

I'm looking forward to getting their data and finding out more about them. I had no idea Shari lived on an island. We should have a meet&greet night on the distantstudybuddy listserv. Everyone has to write one paragraph about why they are distant learners and some other stuff about themselves. Hmmm. I guess I'd have to make something up ... wouldn't want them to know why I'm here ... maybe the meet&greet is not such a good idea after all.

Mom's stress leave is over and she's back at work. Thank God. I don't think I could have handled one more minute of her hovering, trying to be cheerful when I could see all she wanted to do was cry every time she looked at me ... I don't know how long she'll last at work, though. She's lost more weight than I have, she looks like death (no offense, O Immortal One) and

I don't think she's sleeping much by the look of her baggy saggy eyes. Why does that make me feel guilty? It's not like I got sick on purpose.

Was it really just a year ago that I was like everyone else, happily going along just living my life, not feeling like I had to APPRECIATE it? We all get born. We live, we grow up, possibly get married, have babies, grow old, and THEN die. For most of our lives, death should be so far off we don't even have to think about it. I didn't used to have to be grateful that I was still alive. I just was.

Facing your mortality SUCKS!

O Immortal Twin, can you explain—WHY ME?

Well, that's it for this week. I hope not to see you soon.

The mortal one

Form a Hypothesis

Forecast For the Week of
Jan. 29 – Feb. 5
by B.A. Stargazer

♊

Gemini (May 22 – June 21)

February presents challenges and
disruptions, Gemini. Aim for clarity
this week.

From: jselenski
To: cosmicgirl
Subject: Re: Progress Report #1

Dear Kaleigh,

Thank you for submitting your first installment in a timely fashion. It seems you are on the right track and making progress. As for finding the information hard to understand, you didn't choose astrology because you thought it was going to be easy, did you? I certainly hope not. I'm glad to know you are learning something, even if it is on a subject that I still find somewhat dubious. Don't forget to form and clearly state your hypothesis by the next progress report.

Contacting an astrologer is a splendid idea. If you do establish a relationship with her, I hope you will turn in your correspondence as part of your final project. I suspect I would find her comments very enlightening, or at the least, entertaining.

Here's something I want you to think about. Astrologers tell us that it is the position of the sun, the moon, the planets, etc., at the time of a person's birth that determines their personality and character traits. What I wonder, is why is it the moment of birth and not the moment of conception? By choosing the moment of birth, astrologers are implying that at the very moment before birth, a baby is still "a blank slate," right? I think a lot of people would strongly disagree with that implication.

By the way, Kaleigh, I'm pleased that you don't think you'll need an extension on this project. I'll take that as a positive sign that you're still feeling well, all things considered.

Sincerely,

Mr. J. Selenski

… who is not a Scorpio and who cannot figure out why you think I am "intense" or "strong-willed," or even "unpredictable" and "contrary," as you suggested in a previous letter. (No offense taken.) Try again.

From: cosmicgirl
To: blondeshavemorefun
Cc: 2good4u
Subject: data collection

Dear blondie and 2good,

I'm at the "collecting data" stage for my science project on astrology (as well as forming a hypothesis, and gathering information — ongoing) (phew! I'm one busy science student!) and am wondering if you could start sending me your notes (to date) on whether the horoscopes are coming true for you. The third Leo subject has sent me some data — anecdotal (which means a story) — that shows that the weekly horoscope did (in a miraculous way!) fit her week. How about yours? Would you like to share a story or two?

My own horoscope (Gemini) told me to aim for clarity this week. (Have I been clear in this letter? Did I use too many big words? Is my letter too formal? Not formal enough? Do you think I overdo my use of brackets ( ) ?)

Feel free to simply attach your (well-written) notes to your next e-note, but then don't stop taking them! Hopefully this will just be the first of many reporting periods.

Yours in clarity (I hope), and in brackets (for sure!),

Kaleigh

From: 2good4u
To: cosmicgirl
Subject: Re: data collection
Attachment: horoscope notes, batch #1

Leo — **the year ahead:** For some Leos, the next twelve months will contain events that will transform your life for the better. Jupiter increases confidence and helps you make big plans and fulfill them. Sometimes a Jupiter transit will bring fame, and you may make a name for yourself. The only thing you will have to watch with Jupiter in Leo is that you don't become too big for your boots!

Now I ask you, Kaleigh, do you think a modest guy like me could ever become too big for his boots? Never!

This prediction for my coming year is odd. You see, my life is already great! The reason I'm a distant learner is that I'm an actor and am so busy starring in movies that I don't have time to go to school. And this is not on a small scale. If this horoscope had been presented to me three years ago, when I was a struggling actor-wannabe, I would have said Yippee! But the truth is, I've already found fame and have made a name for myself. It just keeps getting better. As you've already guessed, lack of confidence is not something I suffer from. I don't know how this Jupiter fellow will be able to increase it. My adoring fans have already done that.

Now I guess you understand why I couldn't tell you or any of the other distantstudybuddies my name. If I did, everyone on this listserv would inundate me with requests for autographs, and I'd never get my homework done. I'm hoping, Kaleigh, that you'll keep my career a secret. People tend to get so silly when they are corresponding with stars.

Back to the horoscopes. I guess it's too soon to really know if my year will continue to get better, but it appears that it will. I am working on a big movie right now, and as soon as I'm finished on this one, I'm going to be whisked away to the Congo to star in another. (I hope that's not too much information to give you. I wouldn't want you figuring out who I am!) I suppose that means the horoscope is accurate. Perhaps I'll be offered an even bigger role after that—although that would be nearly impossible.

Do you think it's likely that your other Leo guinea pigs will find fame during this Jupiter transit? Maybe my agent should be calling them!

2good

From: cosmicgirl
To: 2good4u
Subject: Re: data collection

2good,

I am stunned. I really am. In fact, at first I was so stunned that

I thought it couldn't be true and that you were making it all up! I waited a day before responding because I thought—knowing you—there'd be a little follow-up note saying Ha ha! Fooled you! But of course that's silly. It's just that it was hard for me to get my head around the fact that I knew (I guess knew/know is the wrong word, but you know (knew!) what I mean!) a famous person. But thank you for taking the time out of your crazy schedule to be a guinea pig in my silly little science project. I really appreciate it. And of course, your secret is safe with me!

Kaleigh
who'd be your #1 fan if she knew who you were!

From: cosmicgirl
To: B.A. Stargazer
Subject: Science Report

Dear Ms. Stargazer,

When I was doing my research on conflicting horoscopes, I came across a funny little story. It goes like this. Lord Vishnu, who was a Hindu god, called all of his astrologers together. He had decided that they had far too much control over his life, so he cast a curse on them. He decreed that no two astrologers would ever again agree on anything.

So now I know why astrologers give conflicting forecasts! LOL! I definitely won't tell Mr. Selenski this story. It would just add fuel to his "I told you so" fire.

I have to admit, Ms. Stargazer, I have been studying the forecasts of other astrologers lately. It's not that I've stopped being your "loyal Gemini fan," but I keep hoping to find one that is more optimistic for Geminis.

Kaleigh Wyse

From: blondeshavemorefun
To: cosmicgirl
Subject: Re: data collection

Cosmic, something really bizarre happened yesterday, and I think a girl may be alive today because of you, the astrologer and me. This is just my first data report to you, but I'm sure it will be the one most strongly supporting horoscopes that you'll ever get from this loyal subject. I can't imagine topping this.

I've never been a horoscope reader, but because of your science project, I read my daily one yesterday and it said, "You may be the hero who saves the day. Your levelheadedness pays off when people confide in you." When I read it I laughed and thought, Yeah, right. Like that ever happens.

Later, I was hanging out in a Jedi chatroom, just yakking with some of my Jedi buds. A girl I met in there asked to speak to me, alone. We moved into a private room and that's when she told me how she'd just taken an overdose (very un-Jedi-like). At first I didn't believe her—she often says stuff just for attention. We yakked some more, but she was starting to make less and less sense. Then she just disappeared without saying goodbye. At first I was sure she was playing around again, but then I remembered the horoscope and I got really worried. But what could I do? I told some of the others in the chatroom about what had happened. We decided we had to do something. Someone knew the town she lived in, so I was able to get a listing of all the high schools there from the internet. I phoned three schools before I found the one she attended. I asked to speak to the principal and I told him what I knew. Thank God he took me seriously. He placed a 9-1-1 call and directed the paramedics to her house. Sure enough, they found her unconscious. I waited and waited. Finally he phoned me back. He told me I'd saved her life.

Is that incredible or what? I still feel shaky about the whole thing, and I'm not prone to the shakes.

The weird thing is, I don't think I would have bothered tracking her down if I hadn't read my horoscope that morning. I mean, what are the chances?? So the question is … do horoscopes appear to come true because we read and act on them? Do we subconsciously look for incidents that would fit the prediction? Or do they come true because the astrologer knew they would? It's the old what-comes-first question, the chicken or the egg?

Cosmic, I have a confession to make. I offered to be one of your guinea pigs just for laughs, but now I'm spooked. In some ways I want to go back to being an innocent non-horoscope-reader so that I can safely continue believing that I'm the only one in control of me. But I doubt that I can do that now.

I'm actually afraid of what I might read tomorrow. What if the astrologer tells me something really bad is going to happen? I'll be a nervous wreck all day!

blondie

From: cosmicgirl
To: blondeshavemorefun
Subject: Re: data collection

OMIGOD! You're so right. That is bizarre. Do you mind if I share your story with the astrologer? I've been emailing her and telling her about my project. I'll ask her your chicken-and-egg question, and if she ever gets around to answering my mail, maybe she'll give you a reply.

I still can't get over what happened to you. You saved a girl's life. How does that feel? What if you hadn't read that horoscope and hadn't made those calls and then found out she'd died! I can't even think about that. But on any other day that is what may have happened. Is it just a coincidence that you read the horoscope on the very day you needed to?

I admit, I do tend to take horoscopes seriously, especially when I like what I read. If I don't like it, or it doesn't seem to fit my life, I try to forget it right away. LOL. But blondie, the data that I've collected so far in this project blows me away. It seems that each of you has read something in one of your horoscopes that is totally about your life or is something that points to what is about to happen to you. Even though I'm a believer, I would never have thought I'd get the kind of results I'm getting, and so quickly. I agree, it's actually a little scary. Right now I'm also afraid of what may happen if I don't like what I read. I don't know if I'll be able to just forget about it — like before—since I heard what happened to you. It's hard to explain, but positive messages are extra important to me at the moment.

Keep on collecting data. This is turning out to be an amazing project.

Kaleigh

From: blondeshavemorefun
To: cosmicgirl
Subject: Re: data collection

Cosmicgirl, your questions have really got me thinking. If I hadn't read the daily horoscope, I wouldn't have "known" that I might be the "hero" that was supposed to save the day, right? Like I said, I thought it was the message in the horoscope that gave me the push to do something, but now I'm wondering... maybe I would have done something anyway. Maybe my conscience would have kicked in. That way the horoscope would still be accurate. I just would never have known that it predicted what I later did. Does that make sense? (It's still the chicken-and-the-egg puzzle.) And if that's the case, what's the point in reading those columns? We're going to do what we're going to do anyway. And I don't believe that all Leos everywhere were heroes yesterday. Why me? Because

I read the prediction? I guess we'll never know, but I suspect I'll take horoscopes a little more seriously from now on, whether I want to or not.

Go ahead and ask the astrologer the chicken & egg question and tell me if she replies.

blondie

P.S. If she had died, I'd probably never know. I would have just wondered about why she was never in the Jedi chatroom anymore. And I may have saved her life, but she's bound to do it again if she doesn't get the help she needs, and there's not much I can do about that.

From: cosmicgirl
To: B.A. Stargazer
Subject: The chicken or the egg?
Attachment: Re: data collection

Dear B.A. Stargazer,

Me again! (I'm the girl doing a science report on astrology, just in case you've forgotten!) I have attached a letter I received from one of my Leo guinea pigs. I'm sending his letter to you because I thought you might like to know how you helped save a girl's life! Do you realize as you write your columns the impact they can have on a person's life? I hope you are proud of yourself!!

The other reason I am attaching his letter is because he asks an interesting question about whether horoscopes come true for a person because they've read them or because they would anyway. Maybe you could even answer his question in one of your upcoming columns.

There's something else I've been wanting to ask you. It's kind of silly, but I'm wondering if there's any way a person can reverse their horoscope if they want to. What I mean is, if my horoscope said something bad was going to happen, could I change that? Could I keep the bad thing from happening?

Anyway, congratulations for helping save the life of that girl!

Your Gemini friend,
Kaleigh

From: cosmicgirl
To: jselenski
Subject: Hypothesis

Dear Mr. Selenski,

I have begun collecting data from my Leo subjects, and the results so far are stunning! For example, one of my subjects read his daily horoscope and was told he would be a hero and save the day. By that evening he had saved a girl's life! It was a truly amazing story. That is just one of a few incredible stories I have collected already. As a result, I've formed a hypothesis and did not want to wait until my next progress report to turn it in.

Hypothesis: The horoscopes written by B.A. Stargazer accurately reflect events in the lives of Leo subjects.

Does that work? I have decided to narrow it down to the horoscopes of one astrologer and in one sun sign in order to eliminate some potentially confusing variables (ie., conflicting forecasts).

Scientifically yours,

Kaleigh Wyse

… and if you're not a Leo, Aquarius or Scorpio, then you must be a Taurus, who is known for being:
persistent—you push your students to work harder
enduring—you put up with a lot of abuse from slacker kids
conventional—you like to do things by the book, i.e., the Scientific Method

----

From: jselenski
To: cosmicgirl
Subject: Re: Hypothesis

Dear Kaleigh,

I sense that you are having more fun with this science project than most of my other students, who have chosen more "conventional" subjects. I'm glad I made the decision to allow you to proceed with this topic.

Your hypothesis is sound. I guess the question would be: Is astrology testable? You will need to prove to me that it is, somehow.

And you can consider this your second progress report. I can sense progress is being made.

Something else to ponder while you collect data... There is a phenomenon known as the Forer effect. Psychologist B.R. Forer found that when given a list of very general personality traits (as in astrology), most people agree that these traits apply exclusively to them, and they don't recognize that these same traits could just as easily apply to almost anyone else.

And another thing: Do you think people seek out the advice of psychics, mediums and astrologers to try to make sense of the thousands of pieces of information we face daily? Is it the combination of hope and uncertainty that creates the need to do this?

Give these ideas some thought, will you?

Sincerely,

Mr. J. Selenski
(who is learning to be less conventional, thanks to you)

P.S. Guess again.

Feb. 4

Dear Twin,

I think I get A++ for clarity this week, don't you? And as for those "challenges and disruptions" that are going to happen in Feb ... I guess it's written in the stars. Can I change that? I don't know. Ms. Stargazer won't answer me! But then, challenges and disruptions don't necessarily have to be bad things, do they? Maybe I just need another shift in the old attitude ...

So, Mr. Selenski is suggesting that those of us who read horoscopes do it because we need to make sense of our world. Now I ask you, what's wrong with that? How does he make sense of it all? How does he explain why BAD things happen to GOOD people? (Like me!) He won't find the answers by reading science textbooks or conducting experiments! Maybe he looks for answers on Discovery Channel. I happen to prefer horoscopes. We know astrology is not just a passing fad. People have been looking to the Cosmos for answers forever. Mr. Selenski lacks faith. I wonder if I should tell him that.

And about those lists of vague personality traits ... well duh! It's the combination of certain traits that describes people. I fit the description of a Gemini perfectly. I do not fit the description of a Leo. Or a Virgo. I think Mr. S. should look a little more closely into how that experiment was conducted. If those people were given the traits of a sun sign other than their own, I'm sure they wouldn't have agreed that it described them. If you mix a random bunch of personality traits together, well, maybe they would see themselves in some, or even most of them. But that's not how it works with astrology. I need to do a better job of educating Mr. S.

I hope next week brings me horoscopes full of messages like "Great things are going to happen to you!" "You are going to meet the man of your dreams!" "This year brings you excellent health!"

That's not wishing for too much, is it, dear twin?

Til next week.

Still mortal.

Experiment

Forecast For the Week of
Feb. 5 – Feb. 11
by B.A. Stargazer

♊

Gemini (May 22 – June 21)

In the weeks ahead, do not let fear rule your life. Be an agent of creativity for yourself and those around you. Communicate, and greater understanding will occur.

From: cosmicgirl
To: blondeshavemorefun
Subject: Re: data collection

Hi blondie,

I emailed the astrologer with your story and the chicken-and-egg question, but I haven't heard back. I'll let you know if I do.

By the way, you said that the girl you saved will probably attempt suicide again if she doesn't get the help she needs, and that there is nothing you can do about that. But blondie, she wouldn't even be here to get help if it hadn't been for you! You can be my hero, my knight in shining armor, any time you like. And I'm picturing you as a guy because I like the idea of being saved by a guy more than by a girl!

Kaleigh

From: starlight
To: cosmicgirl
Subject: Reporting In

Dear Kaleigh,

It just keeps getting better. This week my horoscope said, "You gain energy from participating in outrageous flirtation." Well, that's all the encouragement I needed! I've been emailing back and forth with Chris and Matt. At first we kept it casual, but when Chris started getting more personal, so did I. Now I'm mostly just writing to him. I bet we email back and forth 10 times a day, swapping stories! What a blast! He told me about the time a skunk almost became a stowaway on their boat (oh my god, can you imagine??), and I told him about the time I slept with my window open and woke up when a squirrel scampered across my face! We chat about what we'd like to do once we no longer have to be victims of our parents' dreams. Turns out he doesn't like spending time boating with his any more than I like being imprisoned on this island by mine. We've even shared fantasy escape plans. Now we're making plans to escape together! I know it'll never happen, but the conspiracy's so much fun. And once again that astrologer is right—I'm getting heaps of energy from this. Writing to Chris gives me something to get out of bed for each day. Thanks for doing this project, Kaleigh. Reading the horoscopes gives me permission to do things I might not have done otherwise—like flirt outrageously!

Shari

From: cosmicgirl
To: starlight
Subject: Re: Reporting In

Hi Shari,
Thanks for the report. I'm glad things are going so well between you and Chris. And don't thank me. These things were written in the stars, remember?

Keep the reports coming in!

Kaleigh

From: cosmicgirl
To: B.A. Stargazer
Subject: Science Report

Dear Ms. Stargazer,

I have to apologize for the silly question that I asked in my last letter, the one about reversing your horoscope. Obviously it would take a giant with a huge lung capacity to suck in enough air to exhale hard enough to blow the cosmos around. LOL. I guess it was just wishful thinking on my part.

I've been thinking a lot about something I read in the opening blurb of one of your past columns. You said something about how positive attitudes can create more miracles than wonder drugs. That's nice in theory, but what about a person with a serious illness, like cancer? Do you really think a positive attitude can cure that person? Personally, I put more faith in wonder drugs, but that's just my opinion.

Your Gemini friend,

Kaleigh Wyse

From: 2good4u
To: cosmicgirl
Subject: Re: data collection
Attachment: horoscope notes, batch #2

Leo — the month ahead: If you don't like the role you've been taking on at work, change it. You don't need to keep on doing something that didn't turn out to be what you'd expected.

Well, Kaleigh, after I read this horoscope, I went straight to my director and suggested some changes to the character I've been playing, as well as changes to the story that I thought were necessary. You should have seen his eyes after I explained the problem—as I saw it—to him. It was like a light went on. You're absolutely right! he said. He called everyone together, including the writer, and asked me to explain the changes we had to make. Not one person disagreed with me.

Now I'm thinking … why should I have people (directors, producers) telling me what to do? I should be the director/producer.

Thanks for leading me to this epiphany, Kaleigh.

2good

From: cosmicgirl
To: 2good4u
Subject: Re: data collection

But 2good, you're only a teenager, still in high school! (Well, not actually "in," but you know what I mean.) Don't you think you're a bit too young to be a director or producer?

Kaleigh

From: 2good4u
To: cosmicgirl
Subject: Re: data collection

"As is our confidence, so is our capacity." (William Hazlitt)

From: cosmicgirl
To: 2good4u
Subject: Re: data collection

I guess you'll be a director/producer after all, because you sure do have an overabundance of confidence! (Wanna share some with me?) Just think, soon I'll be able to say I know a famous actor/director/producer! Cool.

Kaleigh

```
------------------------------
```

From: blondeshavemorefun
To: cosmicgirl
Subject: data collection

Hi cosmicgirl,

Today I read my horoscope at the end of the day. (I'm still thinking about the chicken/egg thing.) It said that Leos would be feeling particularly spiritual today. Interestingly, I spent most of the
day chatting in the Jedi room when I wasn't doing schoolwork.
What do you think of that?

blondie

```
------------------------------
```

From: cosmicgirl
To: blondeshavemorefun
Subject: Re: data collection

Aha! We get closer to solving the chicken/egg mystery! Seems you
don't have to read the horoscope first in order to make something
happen!

k.

```
------------------------------
```
From: starlight
To: cosmicgirl
Subject: Reporting In

Hey Kaleigh,

Chris and I have pronounced ourselves "soul-mates." (We'd like to be a lot more, but you know how it is when one of you lives on an island and the other one lives on a boat traveling IN THE WRONG DIRECTION.) Anyway, does that sound "spiritual" to you? Today's horoscope said that we'd be feeling spiritual today.

Shari

```
------------------------------
```
From: cosmicgirl
To: starlight
Subject: Re: Reporting In

It works for me. blondie found his spirituality in a Jedi chatroom. I'll have to check in with 2good.
k.

```
------------------------------
```
From: cosmicgirl
To: 2good4u
Subject: Spirituality

2good, did anything spiritual happen to you today?
k.

From: 2good4u
To: cosmicgirl
Subject: Re: Spirituality

Kaleigh,

Funny you should ask. While in my dressing room, resting, I heard some weird noises coming from the closet. For lack of any other explanation, I decided it must be a ghost. Some people have skeletons in their closets. I have ghosts. Is that spiritual enough for you?

2good

From: cosmicgirl
To: B.A. Stargazer
Subject: Greater Understanding

Dear B.A. Stargazer,

In this week's forecast for Gemini, you suggested we "communicate, and greater understanding will occur." I guess that's one of the reasons I keep writing to you, even though you don't write back. I'm hoping for "greater understanding," so I've decided to tell you even more about some of the stuff going on in my life. Knowing that it's unlikely that we'll ever meet in person, I feel safe sharing this with you.

I do school through correspondence because I have a form of cancer called Ewing's Tumor (the tumor is on the bone in my right leg) and I've been undergoing treatment for it for the past year. I'm in the hospital as much as I'm at home, so it's easier for me to do school this way. I haven't told my distantstudybuddies (other correspondence students) about this because I like the diversion of talking about other stuff with them, but the truth is, I'm really thinking about the disease 24/7. I live it and breathe it. So do the people around me. That could be why my old friends have stopped coming to see me. They just can't handle it anymore.

I've read that I have a 60% chance of surviving this. That is supposed to make me optimistic. I try not to think about that other 40%, but it's hard not to. One of the other patients at the cancer clinic pointed out that if a planeload of passengers were told they had a 60% chance of arriving safely at their destination, everyone would immediately bail. I wish I could bail from this disease.

So, I've had surgery, I've had chemotherapy, but some of the tumor remains. I've now started radiation therapy. As you suggested, I'm trying not to let fear rule my life, but really, how can I not? I'm too young to die!!

By the way, you also said in the last weekly forecast for Gemini that we should be agents of creativity. I definitely think I've been one for my Leo subjects. Each of them is really giving some serious (and not so serious) creative thought to horoscopes. The results have been interesting.

Anyway, I'm sure you wish I hadn't dumped all this on you, but now that I've communicated, I'm waiting for "greater understanding to come."

Your Gemini friend,

Kaleigh

From: starlight
To: cosmicgirl
Subject: Confrontation

Yikes! Today's horoscope said that the time was ripe for a confrontation! I sure hope it isn't with Chris. I'm being very very careful about what I say to him today. Maybe I'll go pick a fight with my dad, get the confrontation thing out of the way so I know it won't happen with Chris.

Shari

From: blondeshavemorefun
To: cosmicgirl
Subject: data collection

Cosmicgirl, after having a major feud with my mom, I read my horoscope for today and was not too surprised that it said the time was ripe for a confrontation. Mind you, the time is always ripe for a confrontation with her. That's the trouble with this distant learning thing. We're both at home all the time. She works at home. I work at home. That's way too much time together. Anyway, you can note another "hit" with the horoscope. And how are you tabulating all this data anyway?

blondie

From: cosmicgirl
To: blondeshavemorefun
Subject: Re: data collection

blondie, I wish you hadn't asked (about tabulating). It's become a nightmare! I have all this wonderful data from you guys (and girl) (girls and guy? you still haven't told me!), but I don't know what to do with it. Each of you has been reporting when there is a "hit," as you put it. That's great, because that is what I set out to prove. But no one tells me when there is no hit. And I think I blew it when I suggested you do daily, weekly, monthly and yearly checks. That just makes it even more complicated! I guess I thought that I'd get better results that way. To be honest, right now I'm tired and I just feel like scrapping this whole project. Tell Mr. Selenski that I quit! Actually, that's not quite true. I'm having fun hearing about each of your lives. I'm getting to know you better than I ever would have otherwise. (I was in need of some new friends.) I'd like you to keep the data coming in. I just don't know what to do with it all.

By the way, why are you a distant learner? If you don't get along with your mom, wouldn't you be better off at school?

k.

From: cosmicgirl
To: jselenski
Subject: Progress Report #3

Dear Mr. Selenski,

About my science project. I have good news and bad news. First the good news. My Leo subjects are sending me lots of data, which records all their "hits." ("Hit" is the word we're using to indicate when a horoscope has come true in some way.) We've had some good conversations about the nature of horoscopes. I have learned a lot about these three studybuddies, and everyone seems to be having fun.

Now the bad news. Do you remember in your last letter you asked me if astrology was testable? At the time I thought it was. I still do. What I can't figure out is how to tabulate all the data I am collecting. Also, I wish I'd narrowed down the scope (how's that for a good scientific word, Mr. Selenski?). You see, my Leo subjects are reading daily, weekly, monthly and yearly horoscopes. I should have just stuck to weekly, or even daily. Then I'd be able to say something like, 2 out of 3 subjects had hits on Feb. 21st, or whatever. As it is, I am drowning in paper and stories around the hits.

And about your sign. You can't be Cancer (sensitive and moody), and I'm sure you're not a Gemini because you don't seem to be anything like me. That really narrows down the field. You must be a Virgo: practical, logical, dedicated and critical. Right?

Going star-crazy,

Kaleigh Wyse

From: jselenski
To: cosmicgirl
Subject: Re: Progress Report #3

Kaleigh,

    I am very pleased with the progress you are making on this project. I'm glad you discovered on your own that the scope (yes, very good word) was too unwieldy. Remember, the Scientific Method is Seven Steps to Discovery. The point of these projects is not simply to come up with a fabulous final report. It is in the process of conducting an experiment that so much can be learned. You thought you were narrowing down the variables by only using one astrologer's forecasts, but now you realize that there were still too many variables. The best way to learn things is by trial and error. Well done!

    Now, more good news. It is not too late to start again. Not with a new topic (scared you for a moment there, didn't I, Kaleigh), but with a fresh start to your data collecting. Don't throw out what you've already collected, but ask your subjects to respond only to their daily horoscopes and you will more easily be able to tabulate the "hits" and "misses."

    Now, about my sun sign. I'm glad you don't think I'm sensitive or moody. And I'm delighted that you think I am practical, logical and dedicated. It's true. I am. But why do you think I'm critical? And maybe I'm more like you than you realize. After all, how well do you know me? How well do you know anyone you meet online? Are we not just a summation of the character traits we choose to show? I once marked a science project on body language. Although it was not the best project I've ever seen (oops, there I go being critical again!), the student did demonstrate that we learn a lot about a person by meeting them face to face and picking up visual clues.

Just something very unscientific to think about.

Yours truly,

Mr. J. Selenski

From: cosmicgirl
To: 2good4u
Cc: starlight; blondeshavemorefun
Subject: Data collection

Dear Leo Subjects,

You have been giving me awesome data for my science project. THANK YOU! Trouble is, you're doing such a good job that I just can't keep track of it all. I've been in touch with Mr. S. and he suggested that we narrow "the scope." From now on, I'm only going to tabulate hits on daily horoscopes. (Forget the weekly, monthly, yearly—way too confusing!) To help me even more, please put the word Hit in the Subject of your email, and then tell me what happened. If there was no hit for you, please write No Hit in the subject. That way I'll know you haven't just forgotten about my silly little project that day. I will set up a graph with days of the week and the number of hits that happened that day. I think that is the proper way to collect scientific data.

Makes sense?

Your star-crazy friend,
Kaleigh

Feb. 11

Dear Twin,

I believe I did just what I was told in this week's horoscope, but I'm no further ahead. I communicated—a lot—with everyone —but what greater understanding do I have? None. SWEET F. ALL! (Sorry, twin, but I'm getting a little aggravated by my lack of understanding, as well as by this tiredness that I just can't do anything about.)

Fear? Oh yeah, I'll just tell myself not to be afraid.

"Kaleigh, don't be afraid."

"Okay. I won't be."

Right.

I'm beginning to wonder if Ms. Stargazer is as wise as I once thought. She's clearly never had a life-threatening disease, or she wouldn't say such stupid things.

But I think I have been a good "agent of creativity." My Leo team has really jumped on board when it comes to my project. Thank God for them. In fact, if it weren't for them ... I better not go there.

Mr. S. is like so wrong about us needing physical clues to get to know a person. I think it's just the opposite. By meeting online, we don't let physical stuff get in the way of getting to know each other. It doesn't matter whether my clothes are cool, or whether I'm tall, short, fat, thin, hairy or hairless. I could have a big nose, buckteeth, zits. It doesn't matter. When you meet online, you get right to the heart of matters, right to what's important. Mr. S. is just old and old-fashioned. His generation has not caught up. He probably thinks he needs to form one of those encounter groups—or whatever they were called—to really chill with his pals. I can just see them, sitting in a circle, the candles are lit, they are meditating... Oh! Now they are astro-traveling! Watch out, Mr. S. Come back! We need you to lead us to greater scientific knowledge! Forget about your feelings—you're a scientist!

All this ranting is tiring. I need another snooze...

Your twin

More Experimenting

Forecast For the Week of
Feb. 12 – Feb. 18
by B.A. Stargazer

♊

Gemini (May 22 – June 21)

Many things depend on how brave you are willing to be. Life is changing. This is the time for spiritual and personal growth. Remain positive.

```
------------------------------
```
From: 2good4u
To: cosmicgirl
Subject: Hit

Today's horoscope for Leos was a good one. Stargazer said, "Relationships pick up momentum, especially love relationships." Did I tell you about my co-star? :)

2good

```
------------------------------
```
From: starlight
To: cosmicgirl
Subject: Hit

Yes! I won't give you the details, but consider today's horoscope to be a big hit with this Leo!

Shari, who just might be in love.

```
------------------------------
```
From: cosmicgirl
To: starlight
Subject: Re: Hit

Shari, are you talking about Chris? How can you be in love with someone you don't even know?! Come to your senses, girl.

k.

From: starlight
To: cosmicgirl
Subject: Re: Hit

Kaleigh, what do you mean by "I don't know him"? We write to each other every day, and he's even phoned me from "port" a couple of times. We share our most intimate thoughts and feelings. How can you say that?!

Shari

From: cosmicgirl
To: starlight
Subject: Re: Hit

Okay, I agree, I'm sure you KNOW him really well. But fall in love? That's entirely different. Don't you think you'd have to go on real dates, stare into each other's eyes, whisper sweet nothings? Seriously, I know people are meeting online, but that just gets things started. I always thought it was when they actually got together—in person—that love could enter the picture. You've only met him once! And he can say anything he wants in his email. None of it is necessarily true. For all you know he has 15 girlfriends, and he tells each of you the same BS. I don't think you should get so carried away, that's all.

Kaleigh

From: starlight
To: cosmicgirl
Subject: Re: Hit

I resent that. I am the only girl Matt writes to. I know that for sure. Maybe you're just jealous.

Shari

From: cosmicgirl
To: starlight
Subject: Re: Hit

Shari, who do you write to, Chris or Matt? You were hot on Chris. Now you're hot on Matt? Or is it both of them?!

Kaleigh

From: starlight
To: cosmicgirl
Subject: Re: Hit

I meant Chris, of course. I don't know why I typed in Matt's name. Just not paying attention I guess. And we ARE falling in love.

Shari

From: cosmicgirl
To: starlight
Subject: Re: Hit

Okay, whatever. It just seems kind of quick, that's all.

k.

From: starlight
To: cosmicgirl
Subject: Re: Hit

Kaleigh, maybe it would be best if you just collected data and didn't comment on your subjects' lives. Otherwise I might have to withdraw from this little experiment of yours.

Shari

From: cosmicgirl
To: starlight
Subject: Re: Hit

I'm sorry, Shari. Really. I won't comment again. Please don't quit the experiment. (But it's not really "little." It's a term project, just in case you didn't know.)

Kaleigh

From: starlight
To: cosmicgirl
Subject: Re: Hit

Kaleigh, you just don't understand because this has never happened to you.

I will stay in the "big" experiment, for now.

Shari

From: cosmicgirl
To: starlight
Subject: Re: Hit

You're right, Shari. I know nothing about love. Unfortunately. And that's not likely to change any time soon, either.

Thanks for hanging in. I think.

k.

From: blondeshavemorefun
To: cosmicgirl
Subject: No hit

From: cosmicgirl
To: blondeshavemorefun
Subject: Re: No hit

Blondie, your last message didn't have a message. Was that on purpose?

k.

From: blondeshavemorefun
To: cosmicgirl
Subject: Re: No hit

Yeah, I figured if nothing happened, I didn't need to elaborate. Too bad, because it would have been nice to have something to say about my love life. Unfortunately, you have to have one in order for it to pick up momentum.

blondie

From: cosmicgirl
To: blondeshavemorefun
Subject: Re: No hit

Yeah, I know what you mean about the love life.

Speaking of relationships, I've had a bit of a fight (misunder-standing?) with one of the other Leo subjects. She's acting super-sensitive. She even threatened to drop out of my experiment, and I thought we were becoming good friends. All I did was say that I thought it was impossible to fall in love with someone you mostly only know online. Wouldn't you agree?

k.

From: blondeshavemorefun
To: cosmicgirl
Subject: Re: No hit

Nice try, Cosmic, but you can't make me take sides in your little dispute with your (not-so-loyal?) Leo subject. All I'll say is this. It seems like a lot of people are meeting online these days, and a lot of those meetings lead to real relationships. If you take the physical appearance quotient out of a new relationship, people tend to be more comfortable with themselves. It becomes a real "meeting of the minds." Besides, I figure I know some of my e-buddies pretty well. Don't you?

blondie

From: cosmicgirl
To: blondeshavemorefun
Subject: Re: No hit

For a guy (person?) who wasn't going to take sides, it seems to me you're pretty onesided! Seriously, I don't really think you can fall in love online. Yeah, you can get past the bull and have great conversations, but what about all those other qualities you'd only see if you were together? What if one of you was a slob and the other one a neat freak? What if one of you was punctual and the other one was always late? What if one of you liked spicy food and the other one liked bland food? What if one liked cuddling, and the other didn't? I could go on and on here, blondie.

Here's an example. I thought I was getting to know Shari pretty well—online. I know, we didn't fall in "love" in the romantic sense, but I thought we'd become real close. She's funny, impulsive, sweet, but I never thought she'd do something so stupid as fall for a guy she's only met once. And I never thought she'd freak when I suggested it might not be love—yet.

And then there's you. I don't even know your real name or whether you're a girl or a guy (though I'm still leaning pretty heavily towards guy). And you never told me why you do school by correspondence. How well do I know you? Not very. So there! :)

k.

From: blondeshavemorefun
To: cosmicgirl
Subject: Re: No hit

I don't know … there's a person I've met online that I'm getting kind of fond of … Maybe Shari's not so irrational after all …
blondie

From: cosmicgirl
To: blondeshavemorefun
Subject: Re: No hit

Omigod, blondie! I would never have thought you'd do something like that! You're my most down-to earth, sensible guinea pig. What is this world coming to! :)

I've been thinking a lot about this getting to know people online. I've got such mixed feelings. Mr. Selenski thinks you need to get clues from a person's body language. I agree, sort of, but now I'm wondering if even a telephone conversation is more telling than an online one. You can hear whether their laughter is real, not just a LOL one. ;) (or a smiley-faced one.) And at least on the phone you can hear the tone someone is using. You can make a statement sound really enthusiastic or really sarcastic, depending on how you say it. Sometimes it's hard to tell online.

Too confusing. It's hurting my tired brain.

k. (who figures you know nothing about this distantstudybuddy)

From: blondeshavemorefun
To: cosmicgirl
Subject: Re: No hit

Oh yeah? I know you're funny, outgoing, and I suspect you're also friendly, kind and lively. Am I close?

blondie

From: cosmicgirl
To: blondeshavemorefun
Subject: Re: No hit

Blondie, WRONG about lively. I'm anything but, today. But thanks for the kind evaluation. You made a lousy day a lot better.

Having a fight with a friend—even if it is online—is so depressing. I've lost touch with my old school friends, so you guys are all that I've got. This stupid science experiment is becoming a drag. I wish I could just forget the whole thing. I'd just like to go to bed and sleep. zzzzzzzzzzzzzzzzzzz

k.

From: blondeshavemorefun
To: cosmicgirl
Subject: Re: No hit

Cosmic, don't worry about Shari. She'll come around. And don't give up on the project! You've invested way too much time and energy into it. Just go take a nap and then get back to it.

Your FRIEND,

blondie

ps why did you lose touch with your school friends?

From: cosmicgirl
To: blondeshavemorefun
Subject: Re: No hit

Thank you, FRIEND. You're sweet. Now I'm off for that snoooooooooze.

k.

P.S. I don't really know why I lost touch with my old friends. Maybe they weren't really "friends" after all. OMIGOD! Maybe you don't even know the people you "know"! I'll go sleep on that depressing thought …

From: 2good4u
To: cosmicgirl
Subject: Hit

This Stargazer babe just doesn't miss! Today's horoscope said, "Arrive on time or don't bother to go at all."

I think I should have stayed home (or at least in my trailer) today.

2good

From: starlight
To: cosmicgirl
Subject: No hit

How can I arrive on time when I have nowhere to go?

Shari

From: blondeshavemorefun
To: cosmicgirl
Subject: No hit

From: cosmicgirl
To: B.A. Stargazer
Subject: Science Project

Dear Ms. Stargazer,

My horoscope this week told me to stay positive. I'm trying, but it's getting really really hard. The radiation is making me SO tired. Being positive requires so much energy. Right now I get exhausted just thinking about staying positive.

The astrology project is suddenly a lot less fun, too. Now that my subjects are just letting me know if they have hits or not, the data collection has become almost boring. It all seems ... I don't know—too scientific. :)

And then there's my subjects. One of them is mad at me. Another one has a hit every single day. (Is that possible? His whole life is beginning to sound a little too good to be true. Hmm. His email name is 2good4u.) The last one hardly has any hits.

I'm tired. Tired from the radiation and fed up with this experiment. I'd like to quit, but that's not thinking very positively, is it? Any chance you can shuffle the stars around for me?

Sorry to be such a downer today. I'll try to think more positively tomorrow, or next week. Maybe. If I'm not too tired.

Kaleigh

From: cosmicgirl
To: jselenski
Subject: Extension

Dear Mr. Selenski,

Do you remember you once offered me an extension on my science project? I'm thinking I might need it now.

Kaleigh

```
------------------------------
```
From: jselenski
To: cosmicgirl
Subject: Re: Extension

Dear Kaleigh,

You take all the time you need to get well. Let me know when you're feeling better again and we'll talk about continuing with your project then.

Mr. J. Selenski

```
------------------------------
```
From: 2good4u
To: cosmicgirl
Subject: Hit

Yesiree. Today we were to receive a "surprising" invitation. Did I ever! And she's pretty hot, too! :)

2good

```
------------------------------
```
From: starlight
To: cosmicgirl
Subject: No hit

```
------------------------------
```
From: blondeshavemorefun
To: cosmicgirl
Subject: No hit

Feb. 18

Spiritual growth? Bravery? Remain positive?

Stargazer can stick it in her ear.

She's got one thing right: Life is changing.

And I don't know if I care anymore.

The twins may be making a teary reunion soon.

Even More Experimenting

Forecast For the Week of
Feb. 19 – Feb. 25
by B.A. Stargazer

♊

Gemini (May 22 – June 21)

New challenges, or new ways of
dealing with old challenges, are
indicated, Gemini. Much goes on
behind the scenes.

From: starlight
To: cosmicgirl
Subject: Hit

Hi Kaleigh,

Big hit! The horoscope said, "you have strong feelings of escapism today." No kidding! I'm seriously thinking of attending school on the mainland next year. I've done everything my parents' way for 15 years. Now it's time to do things my way. What do you think?

Shari

P.S. I'm sorry about my little hissy fit last week. You're right. I overreacted. R we still friends?

From: blondeshavemorefun
To: cosmicgirl
Subject: Hit

Feelings of escapism? Oh yeah. I'd definitely like to escape my mother.

blondie

From: 2good4u
To: cosmicgirl
Subject: No hit

Escape from my perfect life? No way!

2good

From: starlight
To: cosmicgirl
Subject: Hit

And another hit! Stargazer said we would "score" big today. I got the results back from my math test. 98%!! Yay me! Are you taking math? How did you do?

Shari

From: 2good4u
To: cosmicgirl
Subject: Hit

I always "score big." No big surprise there.

2good

P.S. Where are you, Kaleigh? Haven't heard your sweet little "voice" in a while.

From: blondeshavemorefun
To: cosmicgirl
Subject: Hit

Got a great score on my favorite computer game.

blondie

From: starlight
To: cosmicgirl
Subject: Worried

Hey Kaleigh,

Are you still mad at me? Please don't be! Write to me!

Shari

From: blondeshavemorefun
To: cosmicgirl
Subject: ??

Cosmic,

Where are you? I miss chatting with you.

blondie

From: 2good4u
To: cosmicgirl
Subject: Hit

Yep, my "creative juices are flowing," as always.

2good

From: starlight
To: cosmicgirl
Subject: Write to me!

Kaleigh. i'm getting seriously worried about u now. r u ok?

shari

From: 2good4u
To: cosmicgirl
Subject: Hey girl

There's only one small thing wrong with my perfect life. I'm not hearing from you. Wazup?

2good

From: blondeshavemorefun
To: starlight
Cc: 2good4u
Subject: cosmicgirl

u guys are part of Kaleigh's science project, right? have either of u heard from her in the last few days? i'm getting kinda worried. maybe her computer crashed. i hope that's it.

blondie

From: starlight
To: blondeshavemorefun
Cc: 2good4u
Subject: Re: cosmicgirl

i'm worried 2!!! we had a little fight and i thought it was just me she wasn't talking 2. how can we find out what's happening? does anyone have mr. selenkski's e-addresss? i'm not taking science this term.

shari

```
----------------------------
```
From: 2good4u
To: blondeshavemorefun
Cc: starlight
Subject: Re: cosmicgirl

i've been wondering about her 2. i'll contact the good teacher and
c what he knows.

2good

```
----------------------------
```
From: 2good4u
To: jselenski
Subject: Kaleigh

Mr. Selenski,

Do you know why Kaleigh isn't answering emails from her distantstudybuddies? Those of us who are the guinea pigs for her science experiment noticed that she suddenly stopped writing to us.
Very strange for Kaleigh. She's usually real chatty. We're hoping
it's just computer problems.

Lucas Seymour

From: jselenski
To: 2good4u
Subject: Re: Kaleigh

Dear Lucas,

    I'm afraid it isn't computer problems. Although I can't give out personal information about my students, I would like to encourage you and the others to keep writing to Kaleigh, even if she isn't responding. She may need some cheering up.

Mr. J. Selenski

P.S. By the way, it's very good to hear from you, Lucas. Any word on when you're going home?

From: 2good4u
To: jselenski
Subject: Re: Kaleigh

Home. Not a word I relate much to, Mr. S., but I may be released soon, if that's what you want to know. Good behavior and all that.

Lucas

From: 2good4u
To: blondeshavemorefun
Cc: starlight
Subject: Re: cosmicgirl

Soooo … selenski says it's not computer problems, that kaleigh may need cheering up and that we should keep writing to her.

doesn't sound promising, does it? and i was having so much fun being a leo guinea pig, too.

2good

From: starlight
To: blondeshavemorefun
Cc: 2good4u
Subject: Re: cosmicgirl

oh no! that means she's either sick or something really bad has happened in her life. do either of u have her phone number? now i feel even worse about threatening to drop out of her experiment.

shari

From: blondeshavemorefun
To: starlight
Cc: 2good4u
Subject: Re: cosmicgirl

shit!! i figured something must be really wrong. i don't have her number.

blondie

From: 2good4u
To: starlight
Cc: blondeshavemorefun
Subject: Re: cosmicgirl

i don't have her number either. It's a pity, such a sweet, sincere (& gullible) kid, too.

2good

From: blondeshavemorefun
To: 2good4u
Cc: starlight
Subject: Re: cosmicgirl

what do you mean by gullible?

blondie

From: 2good4u
To: blondeshavemorefun
Cc: starlight
Subject: Re: cosmicgirl

i mean that stupid science project on astrology. don't tell me you were taking it seriously? lol! dumb and dumber all over again.

From: blondeshavemorefun
To: 2good4u
Cc: starlight
Subject: Re: cosmicgirl

when i say i'm going to do something, i do it. aren't we supposed to be distantstudyBUDDIES? NOT distantstudyASSHOLES.

From: 2good4u
To: blondeshavemorefun
Cc: starlight
Subject: Re: cosmicgirl

chill out!! it was THIS BUDDY who suggested she do her report on astrology in the first place because she used 2 carry on and on about her horoscope saying this and that. i never thought she'd take me seriously, and i especially never thought selenski would. i even told her that, but she still went for it. just because they buy that horoscope crap doesn't mean i have to.

2good

From: blondeshavemorefun
To: 2good4u
Cc: starlight
Subject: Re: cosmicgirl

2good, i always suspected u were a jerk

From: 2good4u
To: blondeshavemorefun
Cc: starlight
Subject: Re: cosmicgirl

fuck off! i was just having some fun with her. and what difference is it going to make in anyone's life whether i really have hits or not? u guys are 2 pathetic. i'm outta here.

From: starlight
To: blondeshavemorefun
Cc: 2good4u
Subject: Kaleigh Wyse

ENOUGH ALREADY!! Fighting is not going to help Kaleigh.

i suggest we continue writing to her, recording our hits, and when she gets over whatever it is, we just carry on the way it was before. i don't know about u, 2good. maybe it's best if u don't tell her the truth now. it will completely mess up her experiment.

Shari

From: starlight
To: cosmicgirl
Subject: Hit

Hi Kaleigh!

I know you're not writing to me right now, but I'm going to keep sending you my hits and misses. Please write back when you can!

Today my horoscope said that my creative energy would be high, so I tackled my English project. The writing went really well once I got going. Yeah!

Shari

From: blondeshavemorefun
To: cosmicgirl
Subject: Hit

Hi Cosmic,

I had a very creative day, just like Stargazer predicted. You should have seen the sandwich I created for my mother! Peanut butter, mayonnaise, dill pickles, cream cheese, lettuce, sprouts, tomatoes, cucumbers, onion. Who needs to go to one of those fast-food joints for a good sub sandwich?

I've been thinking about how bad I've been, not letting you know whether I'm a girl or a guy. That was mean, and I apologize. Because of that, I've decided to tell you my name. Are you excited?

Are you?
<
<
<
<
<
 Ready now?
<
<
<

Okay. Here it is.
<
<
< ·
<

eimaj.

Oh yeah. I forgot to mention. It's in code. You have to unscramble
the letters. :)

imaje

From: starlight
To: cosmicgirl
Subject: Hit

You are going to be SO proud of me, Kaleigh. My horoscope today said that it would be a good day to "confront the situation that's been bothering you." So guess what I did. I called a family meeting and told my parents that I was attending school on the mainland next year. They very calmly asked why I wanted to go there. I very calmly explained. They were SHOCKED when I told them how unhappy I am on the island. How trapped I feel. I know I've told them—many times!—but I guess I haven't explained it calmly and clearly until now. (Maybe they didn't understand the reason behind my little temper tantrums.)

Anywho—guess what! They said that was fine. That they supported my decision because I'd given it a lot of thought. They suggested I commute next year, and then if everything goes well, they will try to find a family on the mainland for me to live with in Grade 12! Can you believe it? My escape plan is becoming a reality!

I sure miss hearing from you, Kaleigh. I hope everything is okay. Love you lots.

Shari

From: blondeshavemorefun
To: cosmicgirl
Subject: Hit — maybe

Well? Did you guess my name? Did you guess Jamie? So now you know I'm a guy. Or girl. :)

Cosmic, did you notice the subject in this email? The reason I wrote in "maybe" is because I'm not sure if I'm going to do as Stargazer advises. She says to "confront the situation that's been bothering you." Well, the situation I'm going to confront concerns you, and I don't know if I'll actually send this email once I tell you about it. So I'm not sure yet if it is a hit.

Okay, here's the situation. Your other two Leos and I have exchanged a few emails because we were worried about why you'd suddenly stopped contacting us. At one point, the guy called 2good admitted that he hadn't taken your science project seriously. Can you believe it? So now I don't know if you can use the data he gave you. Some of it might not be completely true. Or maybe none of it is. I suspect this will come as a complete surprise to you, and I'm sorry to be the bearer of bad news.

The reason I may not even hit the send button on this email is because I'm not sure if this is the situation I should be confronting. I already confronted 2good. It didn't do me any "good." But I'm wondering if in some way he is right. He implied that what you don't know won't hurt you. Maybe he's right. You could complete the project thinking all your data is legit, score an A+, and Selenski will never know. And neither will you, actually. But 2good, Shari and I will, and I don't feel right being in on this scam.

There's another situation that I haven't confronted, and that is to ask you directly why you've stopped writing to us. I'm super worried about you. Mr. Selenski won't tell us what's wrong, but we do know your computer is working. Please write to me. Just one word is all I need.

Jamie, who now has to decide whether to hit send or not.

Long pause.

Long pause.

Thinking.

Considering.

Here it goes.

Feb. 25

Writing to an imaginary twin was so stupid. What was I thinking? From now on, it's Dear Diary. Oh yeah, that's way less stupid. Why do I write at all? Bad habit.

And yep, the astrologer was bang on this week. The gang was talking about me "behind the scenes." But then, who cares? Not me.

Record and Analyze Data

Forecast For the Week of
Feb. 26 – March 4
by B.A. Stargazer

Ⅱ

Gemini (May 22 – June 21)

You will be facing a solar low this
week. Take things slowly, save
your energy. This is a good time
for reflection and meditation.
A stranger is attracted to you.

To: B.A Stargazer
From: cosmicgirl
Subject: Science Project

Dear Ms. Stargazer,

I think I told you that I've been getting radiation treatment for the past few weeks. Talk about a solar low. It's not as bad as chemo, and at first I didn't feel much, but now I'm completely zapped. With my energy gone, it's hard to get interested in anything. Things I used to care about don't seem important anymore. Some days it's hard to remember why I even want to get well.

I decided to write to you today to try to sort out some of my thoughts. Do you remember how, when I first started my report and experiment on astrology, I was so excited? That was in the lull between chemotherapy and radiation. I was feeling okay and the project seemed to have such possibilities. Now I'm having trouble remembering what the big deal was.

I first became interested in astrology about a year ago when I found out about my tumor. There was a lot of anxious waiting around for tests etc. at the cancer clinic. I remember flipping through a newspaper one day and spotting your Sun Signs column. I'll never forget what the message for Gemini was that day. You said, "Miracles happen when we focus as much on our dreams as we do on our fears."

I only had one dream, and that was to get cured, so I began to focus on that. I didn't know how you knew what I was about to go through, but somehow I felt sure you did, and that you wrote that specifically for me. I was pretty naïve, looking back on it, but I silently recited that message before surgery, after surgery and then throughout my chemo treatments, even when I got so sick I couldn't get out of bed. I recited it while standing in front of the mirror, combing my hair and seeing the huge bald spots appear as my hair fell out in clumps. I continued to recite it even when all my hair was gone, and when I had so many sores in my mouth I couldn't eat anything. Believing in the possibility of miracles got me through that time, and every day I would read my horoscope, looking for hope in what often seemed like a hopeless situation. I was sure I would get well if I continued to focus on my dreams.

Well guess what. The miracle didn't happen after all. When I found out that I still wasn't cured after all that horrible chemo, I got mad and decided to give up on horoscopes. That's when I discovered I'd become addicted to them. I couldn't not read them. Have you ever heard of that before? I've heard of gambling addictions, alcohol and drug addictions, but horoscope addictions? Oh brother.

My science project is on hold. I took a break because I was so tired. I stopped answering my subjects' emails because it took too much energy to pretend to be a fun, happy-go-lucky kind of Gemini. Now I've been told that one of my subjects may have been "faking" his data. I'd begun to suspect as much. So what should I do? Finish the experiment with just two subjects? I suppose I could fake all the data and write the report any way I want to. Mr. Selenski would never know. Whatever, it just doesn't seem worth the trouble. It's hard to care about one stupid school project when I may not even be alive a year from now.

Kaleigh Wyse

From:cosmicgirl
To: jselenski
Subject: Extension

Mr. Selenski,

I have decided not to complete my project after all. Things got too complicated near the end, and now I don't really think it's worth it. The whole thing was a stupid idea. I'll accept the zero I get.

Kaleigh Wyse

From: jselenski
To: cosmicgirl
Subject: Re: Extension

But Kaleigh, I'm afraid I won't allow you to give up. You were doing a terrific job, and even if something did go amiss with your data collection, you just need to explain to me what happened in your written report. That's all part of it. Science experiments are never without their hiccups.

There's another reason you can't quit on me, Kaleigh. The truth is, I'm actually becoming interested in astrology! (Please don't tell anyone. I'd lose my reputation as a levelheaded, no-nonsense, fact-gathering kind of guy.)

And there's one more reason you can't quit on me. You still haven't discovered my sun sign.

Mr. J. Selenski

From: cosmicgirl
To: jselenski
Subject: Re: Extension

But Mr. Selenski, I'm so tired.

Kaleigh

From: jselenski
To: cosmicgirl
Subject: Re: Extension

Dear Kaleigh,

You're forgetting that I have endless patience. (Clue: which sun sign is so patient?) You can finish this project whenever you're feeling well again. When the treatment is finished you will get your energy back. That is a fact. (And you know I don't mess around with facts.) So hang in there. This too shall pass, as they say.

Mr. J. Selenski

From: starlight
To: cosmicgirl
Subject: Hit

Hi Kaleigh,
I hope that whatever is keeping you from writing is getting better.
I miss you!

I just keep on getting hits with my daily horoscopes. Today Leos were to "feel some tension or distress as we try to figure out which way to go." This is so true. I can't go into details right now, but I have done something really stupid, and now I'm having trouble deciding how to get myself out of this mess!

Guess what. Now that my parents have "discovered" how unhappy I am on this island, they are trying to improve the situation. They're researching activities I can do off the island, while still remaining a resident. For example, they've found an art camp for me to go to during spring break. It is a five-night camp, and they feel it will give me the "exposure to other teenagers" that I've been "pining" for. Whatever, I'm really looking forward to it!

Please write to me when you can!

Shari

From: blondeshavemorefun
To: cosmicgirl
Subject: Hit—maybe

Kaleigh,

I'm afraid I'm doing it again. I won't know whether I have a hit today until I decide whether to send this email.

I've been thinking about you a whole lot. I need to know why you "disappeared" so quickly. I can only think that you're really really sick. Or you lost all your fingers in an accident. Or you're depressed. My mom gets very quiet when she's depressed. Could that be it? You always seemed like the opposite of a depressed kind of person, but as you pointed out yourself, we can create whoever we want to be when we're online, right?

That's why I've decided to finally come clean with you. It's been fun playing these little games (guess my name, my gender, etc.), but I'm hoping that if I tell you the truth about me, maybe you'll tell me what is going on with you.

So, I am James Robert Hopkins. I am a 16-year-old white male. (Very white.) I live at home with my mom. I have no brothers or sisters. My dad lives with his new wife in another city.

That's about it. Pretty dull, huh? It was more fun being a mystery person.

Whatever.

Please let me know if you're even out there. I won't bother writing if you're not reading.

Jamie

From: cosmicgirl
To: blondeshavemorefun
Subject: Re: Hit — maybe

Jamie,

Do you realize that's the first time you've used my real name? And this is the first time I've used yours. It feels like a defining moment, somehow. :)

I'm sorry I "disappeared." Can't explain. Not yet anyway. Thanks for being there.

Kaleigh

From: blondeshavemorefun
To: cosmicgirl
Subject: Re: Hit — maybe

THANK GOD YOU'RE ALIVE!

I like that defining moment thought. I like it a lot.

Okay, now that I know you're at least reading this stuff, I'll keep writing. I've quit tabulating my hits and misses because without you responding, I'm not sure you're even keeping track. I am still reading the horoscopes, though. It does become an obsession.

Things I've been wondering:

Is whatever it is that is keeping you from writing, the same thing that made you decide to do school by correspondence?

Are each of us distantstudybuddies hiding behind our computer screens for some reason?

Did that astrologer ever reply to you about the chicken/egg thing?

Jamie

From: blondeshavemorefun
To: starlight
Cc: 2good4u
Subject: Re: Kaleigh Wyse

Just wanted you guys to know that Kaleigh really is still reading her email, even if she isn't writing. I'm pretty sure she still has all her typing fingers, so she's probably sick or sad or something.

Anyway, I think she'd appreciate hearing from you, even if you're not tracking your hits and misses anymore.

Jamie (formerly known as blondie)

From: starlight
To: cosmicgirl
Subject: Recording hits

Hi Kaleigh,

I'm wondering if you still want me to record my hits. Since you've stopped writing, I thought you may have quit collecting data, too. Yes? No?

I sure miss you. Did you write to Blondie (Jamie)? He seems to know something I don't. I'm jealous!

Shari

From: 2good4u
To: cosmicgirl
Subject: hit

Kaleigh—wherever you are—keep your fingers crossed for me. Stargazer said "leos would be rewarded." Guess what? I'm being nominated for an academy award.

2good, as always.

From: cosmicgirl
To: blondeshavemorefun
Cc: starlight; 2good4u
Subject: Data collection

Hi guys,
It's me. I'm back, sort of. Just dropping in to tell you not to bother collecting data anymore. I'll just use what I've got, if I decide to even finish the stupid project.

Sorry I haven't been in touch. I just lost interest in the whole thing. I always did think science sucked. I've decided astrology sucks too.

Thanks for trying to help me out with the project. You're off the hook now.

Take care,

Kaleigh

From: blondeshavemorefun
To: cosmicgirl
Subject: Re: Data collection

Hey! You get me hooked on this stuff and then up and quit! No fair. Why do you think astrology sucks?

Jamie

From: starlight
To: cosmicgirl
Subject: Re: Data collection

Hey Kaleigh, I'm sorry about the astrology project. What happened? I thought you were really into it.

I hope we're still friends. I really want to be.

Shari

From: cosmicgirl
To: starlight
Subject: Re: Data collection

I suppose we're still friends. But really, how close can friends be when it's all online? Oops, I'm sorry. You fell in love online, didn't you?

k.

From: starlight
To: cosmicgirl
Subject: Re: Data collection

What do you mean "how close can friends be online?" I thought we were becoming really good friends! But, come to think of it, friendships have to be give and take. I see now that I did all the "giving." I told you about my life, but you never told me anything about yours. I don't even know why you're a distant learner.

Maybe if you'd shared more with me, told me why you really quit the project, our friendship could've grown. You seem to have changed. I didn't have to meet you in person to figure that out.

Goodbye Kaleigh. It was nice knowing you (or not).

Your ex-friend,

Shari

From: cosmicgirl
To: starlight
Subject: Re: Data collection

Shari, do you really believe that if I told you, through email, more about myself, that we'd become better friends? I could tell you anything I wanted and you'd have no way of knowing if it were true. What's the point?

k.

From: starlight
To: cosmicgirl
Subject: Re: Data collection

You know, you're right. It's hard to know what to believe, isn't it? And I know 2good must have made you suspicious.

Well, guess what. You're right about me, too. I am not worthy of being your friend, online or off. There never was a Chris. Or a Matt. I made them up.

Shari, the online liar

From: cosmicgirl
To: 2good4u
Subject: Data collection

2good,

I know that some (all?) of the data you gave me was made up. The whole project was quite the joke, wasn't it?

Just thought you should know that I know.

Kaleigh

From: 2good4u
To: cosmicgirl
Subject: Re: Data collection

hey, we had fun, doncha think? i really enjoyed being a famous movie-star stud, if only in my mind. And i'd started to fantasize about you, too. Sweet, sweet Kaleigh. i'm sorry my cover was blown so early in the game.

So who are u, really? i sense you're not quite as sweet and happy-go-lucky as i thought. why do u do school by correspondence?

2good

From: cosmicgirl
To: 2good4u
Subject: Re: Data collection

Why would I tell you anything?
kaleigh

From: 2good4u
To: cosmicgirl
Subject: Re: Data collection

Because u think I'm clever and funny and stud-like. And u have the hots for me.

2good

From: cosmicgirl
To: 2good4u
Subject: Ha!

i needed a laugh. thanks.

k.

From: cosmicgirl
To: blondeshavemorefun
Subject: Liars

So Jamie, i just found out that Shari's a liar 2. My whole project was a complete farce. i feel like such a fool.

Anything u want to confess? Did u really save a girl's life? Probably not. i don't know what 2 believe anymore.

Kaleigh.

From: cosmicgirl
To: B.A. Stargazer
Subject: Science Project

Ms. Stargazer,

I've finished the treatments, but still feel gross. I won't know for months or even years whether the radiation worked or not. Even if the tumor appears to be gone, the cancer may have spread to other parts of my body. Not knowing is killing me faster than the cancer. And the treatments may have made me sterile. And they may have weakened my heart. Isn't that just grand?

Everything is wrong. My real-life friends are gone. My online friends are just a bunch of liars. For a while I used you and your horoscopes to give me hope, but now I realize how stupid I was. Mr. Selenski tried to warn me, but I wasn't listening. I guess I didn't want to hear.

I can't believe I've been writing to you like this. You must have had a good laugh. And here I am doing it again.

You won't be hearing from me anymore.

Kaleigh Wyse

March 4

I DON'T WANT TO DIE!!!! I DON'T WANT TO DIE!!!! I DON'T WANT TO DIE!!!! I DON'T WANT TO DIE!!!! I DON'T WANT TO DIE!!!! I DON'T WANT TO DIE!!!! I DON'T WANT TO DIE!!!! I DON'T WANT TO DIE!!!! I DON'T WANT TO DIE!!!! I DON'T WANT TO DIE!!!! I DON'T WANT TO DIE!!!! I DON'T WANT TO DIE!!!! I DON'T WANT TO DIE!!!!

I must be getting my strength back. It was easier not to care either way, to lose the fear. It's back, big time. Shit. What a friggin roller coaster.

I luv my mom. I do I do I do. BUT I NEED HER TO GET OUT OF MY LIFE FOR A WHILE!! *Just the way she looks at me makes me crazy. All the pampering and the fussing and and and!!!!!!!! Even Dad seems to avoid her.*

What have I done to their lives?

I just want to go back to the way I was, before cancer!! Is that too much to ask?

Obviously it is. I'll never be that Kaleigh again.

I feel like such an idiot, being strung along by shari and what's his fat face. And writing to that astrologer? What was I thinking! Writing in this journal is almost as stupid, but at least no one else is reading it. I guess if I had someone, ANYONE, to talk to I wouldn't need this.

Life sucks. Even the word "life" is phony. It sounds active. Full of possibility.

It isn't. I know that now. For a while we are tricked into feeling like it is, that the "sky's the limit," that only our attitudes can hold us back, that miracles are possible. Just another pack of lies.

More Recording and Analyzing

Forecast For the Week of
March 5 – March 11
by B.A. Stargazer

♊

Gemini (May 22 – June 21)

Listen with your heart. Forgive.
Don't give up hope and never
think that you are alone. We
are all together and much
closer than we know.

From: jselenski
To: cosmicgirl
Subject: Science Discovery

Dear Kaleigh,

Just checking in to see how you're feeling.

By the way, last night I was reading of a tremendously interesting science discovery that made me think of you. It seems some researchers were trying to determine exactly how much a person's outlook/attitude affects their health. These researchers took swabs from the inside of people's mouths and studied the cells found there. People with positive outlooks had cells that showed their immune systems were working well. The cells from people who were depressed indicated their immune systems were not functioning at all well.

So, Kaleigh, keep on thinking positivly and you'll strengthen that immune system of yours, which, in turn, will help you get well.

Mr. J. Selenski

From: cosmicgirl
To: jselenski
Subject: Re: Science Discovery

Dear Mr. Selenski,

Maybe those researchers have it backwards. It could be that having a weak immune system makes a person depressed, not the other way around. It's a lot easier to think positively when you're feeling well. And besides, I don't know if there's a connection between developing a tumor and having a weak immune system.

Thanks anyway.

Kaleigh

From: jselenski
To: cosmicgirl
Subject: Success!

Kaleigh,

What brilliant critical thinking skills you've developed! You're absolutely right about that research on immune systems and thinking positively. Was it me who taught you to think like that? Oh dear. I guess that would be rather presumptuous of me to presume, wouldn't it? (There you go, another personality clue to my sun sign. Presumptuous.)

That said (and you may be right), what have any of us got to lose by at least trying to think positively? Scientific research has shown a correlation between positive thinking and good health, and if we at least attempt to see the good around us instead of the bad, we'll feel temporarily better, don't you think? It works for me, anyway.

And you forgot to tell me how you're doing. Well?

Mr. J. Selenski

From: cosmicgirl
To: jselenski
Subject: Re: Success!

Mr. Selenski,

The treatments are over and I feel a little less tired. My science project is a mess, though. I'll spare you the ugly details, but the data I collected is a bunch of crap. You wouldn't want me coming to false conclusions about horoscopes and astrology, would you?

I'm resigned to a zero on the project. I'm thinking I may even drop out of school and do something fun for a change. If my life is going to be short, it might as well be sweet.

Kaleigh

From: jselenski
To: cosmicgirl
Subject: Re: Success!

Kaleigh,

I can't believe you'd quit school. You have forced me to preach to you one of my most famous lectures.

Lecture #467

In the face of adversity (and no one is spared some truly difficult times in life) we can decide whether we are going to give up or take that proverbial bull by the horns and get on with it. Not one of us knows what tomorrow will bring. We have little control over our circumstances, but we can control our thoughts.

Here endeth the lecture.

Seriously, Kaleigh, I know you feel helpless when it comes to the cancer, but you have today. And you can plan for the future. Don't give up now. You're almost through the worst of it.

Mr. J. Selenski

From: cosmicgirl
To: jselenski
Subject: Re: Success!

Believe me, Mr. Selenski, I've been holding tight to those bull's horns, but sometimes I feel like I'm on a bucking bronco.

Okay, I won't quit school, yet. But if I find out I still have the tumor, I'm out of here.

Kaleigh

From: jselenski
To: cosmicgirl
Subject: Re: Success!

That's my girl!!

And please continue to work on the science project. Report to me what you learned in your research and what the data — no matter how untrustworthy—would lead you to believe about horoscopes. Don't worry about progress reports and what not. Just work on a final project.

Mr. J. Selenski

From: blondeshavemorefun
To: cosmicgirl
Subject: Re: Liars

Hey Kaleigh,

r u suggesting i might be a liar 2? i resent that! i know u have a right to be ticked off at 2good and now at shari, too, but i have been completely honest with u. i did make that phone call and that girl was rushed to emergency because of my call. what i don't know for sure is whether i would have done it if i hadn't read my horoscope that day.

i can't believe you'd think i'd lie to u.

jamie

From: cosmicgirl
To: blondeshavemorefun
Subject: Re: Liars

Jamie,

Why should I believe you? You can tell me anything you want, just like shari and 2good did. I don't know you. I will never know you. If I could look you in the eyes and hear you say that you were telling the truth, then I might believe you. As it is, I can't trust anything online anymore.

I'm sorry. I thought I liked you.

Kaleigh

From: blondeshavemorefun
To: cosmicgirl
Subject: Re: Liars

That's crap, Kaleigh, and you know it. Can't you just tell from our messages that I'm sincere? What motivation would I have to lie to you?

jamie

From: cosmicgirl
To: blondeshavemorefun
Subject: Re: Liars

What motivation did 2good and shari have? They lied just for the fun of it. And maybe you are too.
kaleigh

From: blondeshavemorefun
To: cosmicgirl
Subject: Re: Liars

Kaleigh, i don't know why i feel compelled to make you believe me, but i do. i don't give up on friends so easily, and neither should you.

Here's some more honesty.

The reason i do school by correspondence is because i'm albino. That's why i go by blondie. It's a nice nickname. Most of the names i've been called aren't. i don't look "normal" and can't handle the constant reminder of that at high school. It's much easier 2 hide behind this computer screen.

i didn't want you to know because i thought it would scare you off. i like you, and i do believe in online relationships. But i guess it won't happen now.

So, do you think i'd lie about this?

jamie

From: blondeshavemorefun
To: cosmicgirl
Subject: Re: Liars

Kaleigh, are you there?

jamie

From: blondeshavemorefun
To: cosmicgirl
Subject: Re: Liars

kaleigh, i tell you my biggest secret, and you haven't written back. is it because you can't handle that i'm albino?

jamie

From: cosmicgirl
To: blondeshavemorefun
Subject: I'm so sorry

Jamie, I'm sorry. :(I've been so embarrassed I just didn't know how to respond. I should have known that you were telling the truth. And if you think you don't look "normal," you should see me! I lost all my hair recently (chemotherapy) and now it's growing in like peach fuzz all over my head.

Now I know what you meant when you said you were "very white." I thought it might be a racist comment or something. Lol.

Can we start again? (I hope you won't change your mind about me now that you know I'm practically hairless.)

Kaleigh

From: blondeshavemorefun
To: cosmicgirl
Subject: Re: I'm so sorry

Kaleigh,

Thanks for being honest with me, 2. I figured u must be sick with something quite serious. How are u doing?

jamie
ps At least your hair will grow in. I'll be albino forever.

From: cosmicgirl
To: blondeshavemorefun
Subject: Re: I'm so sorry

Hi Jamie,

I'm actually starting to feel a bit better. I've finally finished radiation treatment and now I'm not as tired all the time like I was for a while, but I just can't get back my ... I don't know. My SELF! I feel like someone else, not me anymore. I used to be one of those people who'd wake up each morning looking forward 2 the day.

(Well, after the drowsy part wore off. You know what I mean.) When I was first diagnosed, I'd wake up happy, as usual. And then, WHAM! I'd remember. It was such a shocking jolt. I'd try to go back to sleep, where I could forget, but that was impossible. Why me? I kept asking. I didn't do anything wrong!! I'm a nice person!!! Why couldn't this happen to a not-so-nice person??? There's enuf of them around!

I also began waking up in the middle of the night, soaked in sweat but shaking at the same time. Was it going to hurt? Would the chemo make me sick? Would I lose my hair? Was I going to die? What did death feel like? Why me why me why me!!!!!

One time I woke up from an awful nightmare where I'd been lying in a coffin, dressed in a long white dress. My friends were all looking down on me with sad faces. I wanted to scream, "I'M NOT DEAD! I'M STUCK IN THIS BODY BUT I'M NOT DEAD!" but my mouth wouldn't open and I couldn't move. It was awful. I got out of bed and went down to the kitchen to get something to drink. That's when I heard an odd noise coming from the basement. At first I was scared, but then I realized it was not the kind of sounds a burglar would make. I crept down the stairs and saw a light in my dad's workshop. The noise I heard was him crying! Deep, horrible sobs.

It just broke me up. My mom and I had been doing lots of crying, but my dad was always strong for us. That night I learned his secret. He was crying when he thought we couldn't hear him. That confirmed my fears. If Dad was crying, he must know I was going to die. Dad wouldn't cry otherwise. He would always hang onto hope.

These days I wake up and feel nothing. I'm not dead yet, but emotionally I guess I am. Well, maybe not completely, but pretty close. It's been a long haul. Everyone keeps telling me to "think positive." It's so easy to say, but not at all easy to do. And I hate it when people tell me everything is going to be okay. No one knows that! It just pisses me off when they say it. I know they are trying to help, but it doesn't. It just makes me wish it was them who was sick.

Radiation was my last hope for beating the cancer. Cross your fingers for me.

(And I bet you're wishing you never asked me how I was doing. Lol.) But you know, I just realized that it feels really good to talk to someone (a REAL person) about all this.

Anyhow, now that my energy is coming back, I'm missing my astrology project. It was fun connecting with you guys, even if 2/3rds of the data was a pack of lies. Now my days are long. There's no "fun." No "connections."

I've never known an albino person before. You're missing the color in your skin, hair and eyes, right? Why is that so awful? I always wanted to be blonde.

Kaleigh

From: blondeshavemorefun
To: cosmicgirl
Subject: Re: I'm so sorry

What we're missing is called pigmentation. I wear really thick glasses, which I hate. I'm practically blind, but I guess being albino's not so bad. Especially when I hear what it's like to have cancer. It's weird how we all work so hard to establish our individuality, but basically what we really want is to look like Brad Pitt, right? I've actually been thinking about going back to school. Now that I'm older I might be able to handle it better.

Do you ever wonder why Shari and 2good faked their data? Maybe you should ask them.

jamie

P.S. I'm not sorry I asked how u r!! Thanks for telling me everything. I hope you know I care. And I'm glad you think I'm a "real" person.

From: cosmicgirl
To: blondeshavemorefun
Subject: Re: I'm so sorry

Jamie,

That's so good that you're thinking of going back to school. Best to face your fears, right? That's what everyone keeps telling me.

I think I will contact Shari and 2good. Thanks. And thanks for caring, and bringing a lump to my throat!

k.
and NO, I do NOT want to look like Brad Pitt, thank you very much!
And YES, you're real—in lots of ways—but what I meant was that I'd been doing a lot of writing to imaginary people. Sounds stupid, I know. Long story.

From: cosmicgirl
To: 2good4u
Subject: just wondering …

why you made up all that data for my astrology report? How come you didn't just do it the way you were supposed to?

Kaleigh

From: 2good4u
To: cosmicgirl
Subject: Re: just wondering …

nice 2 hear from u again kaleigh. have u gotten over your little snit? just needed 2 hear from me again?

i told you why. i just wanted 2 have fun.

2good

From: cosmicgirl
To: 2good4u
Subject: Re: just wondering ...

Is your life so dull that the only fun you have is creating online identities?

k.

From: 2good4u
To: cosmicgirl
Subject: Re: just wondering ...

Ooh, Kaleigh. You're getting a little snarky! You're definitely not the sweet little thing i imagined u as. 2 bad. Though maybe now i can re-imagine u as a hot little thing instead. And still hot for me, 2.

Did i mention i've been missing u?

2good

From: cosmicgirl
To: 2good4u
Subject: Re: just wondering ...

C'mon, 2good. Just be serious for one minute. What are you hiding?

k.

From: 2good4u
To: cosmicgirl
Subject: Re: just wondering …

Wouldn't u like to know.

2good

From: cosmicgirl
To: 2good4u
Subject: Re: just wondering …

Oh! So you are hiding something. Jamie suggested all of us distantstudybuddies probably are.

And if I had known you weren't going to take my project seriously, I could have found someone who would have. Then I'd be able to complete it. Are you even a Leo??

k.

From: 2good4u
To: cosmicgirl
Subject: Re: just wondering …

What difference does it make whether i'm a Leo? Will it change anything in the great scheme of things? i think not. u should take life a little less seriously, Kaleigh.

And of course blondie's right. We r all hiding something. Otherwise we'd b out living our lives instead of cowering behind our computer screens.

2good

From: cosmicgirl
To: 2good4u
Subject: Re: just wondering …

You might take life a little more seriously if you were in my shoes.

So why aren't you out living your life?

k.

From:2good4u
To: cosmicgirl
Subject: Re: just wondering …

Because I'm incarcerated. Imprisoned. Confined. Detained. Locked up. Put away. That's my excuse. And yours?

2good

and if I were in your shoes — girl shoes — I'd definitely be taking life less seriously. How many serious drag queens do you know?

From: cosmicgirl
To: 2good4u
Subject: Re: just wondering …

Incarcerated? You expect me to believe that? Right.

Kaleigh

who doesn't know any drag queens, serious or otherwise.

From: 2good4u
To: cosmicgirl
Subject: Re: just wondering …

No, I guess you wouldn't believe it. Imagine YOU corresponding with a PRISONER! God forbid.

u didn't answer me. Y R U hiding behind your computer?

2good

From: cosmicgirl
To: 2good4u
Subject: Re: just wondering …

Why should I tell you, 2good? You never tell me anything.

Kaleigh

From: 2good4u
To: cosmicgirl
Subject: Re: just wondering ...

Okay. Then I'll just have to guess. Let's see ... You're a princess living in an ivory tower? No. I've heard some very unprincess-like thoughts from you.

Your daddy's a billionaire and u keep him company while he jets around the world, making and breaking deals. No, that can't be it either. Daddy would just buy u a teacher to come along if that was the case.

i know you're not an actress, because u were far too impressed when u thought i was an actor. Could u be a model? u could be strutting down a ramp in paris right now. God, i hope not. Those girls are way too skinny for this prisoner. i like a little flesh on my girls.

Well, am i getting close?

2good

From: cosmicgirl
To: 2good4u
Subject: Re: just wondering ...

Real close, 2good. In fact, you're almost there ...
k.

From: cosmicgirl
To: starlight
Subject: lies

Shari, I've been wondering....

Why did you make up all that stuff about Chris and his brother? Do you really live on an island? Did you ever read your horoscopes?

I'm not trying to be mean and stir things up again, and you don't have to answer me, obviously. I'm just trying to sort stuff out.

It's been almost a year since I went to a real school. There's lots of stuff I don't miss about it, but I do miss having friends. I know you mentioned that you wanted to go to school in some of your letters. I really believed that you knew how it felt to be cut off. Even though I told you about the not-so-good parts of school, I could still identify with how you felt.

Anyway, I won't blame you if you don't answer this.

Kaleigh

From: starlight
To: cosmicgirl
Subject: Re: lies

Kaleigh, I don't expect you to believe me, but everything I told you is true, except the stuff about the boys.

I've been racking my brains trying to figure out why I started telling that stupid story. I'm not a liar. That's the first lie I can ever remember telling. I guess I told that one because I didn't want you to know how boring and stupid my life is. And it really is. So when I read my horoscope that first day and it said something about people noticing me more than usual, well, I just knew that wasn't going to happen here. My mom and dad are so caught up in their work that they don't notice me. I hardly ever see anyone else. I didn't want you to know that. I wanted you to think I was interesting. So I started fantasizing about what I'd really like to happen and who I'd really like to notice me. That's when I dreamt up that story. Telling it took me away from the reality of my boring life. It was fun.

Anyway, now you know. I'm sorry I told you lies, but I'm not really sorry I created Chris. It gave me something to think about, other than my crappy life. I miss him. lol

Shari

From: cosmicgirl
To: starlight
Subject: Re: lies

ok, then how come you got so ticked off when i suggested that you couldn't fall in love with an online guy?

are you really going to go to school on the mainland next year?

Kaleigh

From: starlight
To: cosmicgirl
Subject: Re: lies

I've been wondering that myself. Maybe it was because I was beginning to feel so ridiculous and guilty about carrying on the charade for so long. I didn't know how to get out of it. Maybe I thought you were starting to disbelieve me — especially cuz I couldn't even keep their names straight! Maybe I really wanted it to be true. I just don't know. I feel totally stupid now.

Did you tell the others about what I did?

Yes! I really am going to school on the mainland next year. It's confirmed. I've had an interview with the principal and taken an English test. Believe me, Kaleigh, I really didn't lie to you about anything else.

It feels good to be writing to you again. I hope you feel the same. And I hope that you'll forgive me.

So, now that you know about how boring and stupid my life is, why don't you tell me something about you? I'm sure I win the prize for having the dullest life.

Shari

P.S. What are you going to do about the science project?

From: cosmicgirl
To: starlight
Subject: Re: Lies

I don't know what to do about the project. I tried to get out of doing it at all, but Mr. S. wouldn't let me off the hook. I'm going to have to make up something.

Shari, I did tell Jamie that you'd lied to me, but I didn't tell him any more than that. I was just mad and accused him of lying 2.

I have missed writing to you. It's lonely doing school by correspondence, isn't it?

k.

From: starlight
To: cosmicgirl
Subject: Re: Lies

Kaleigh… I'm glad that we're becoming friends again and all that …

BUT YOU STILL HAVEN'T TOLD ME ANYTHING ABOUT YOU!!!!

:)
Shari

March 11

I just read my last few journal entries, and I realize something's changing. I don't feel quite so heavy, so empty. Is it the cosmos, the stars, or just that the radiation has been finished for a while? Maybe both. Or do I dare hope that it's because I've been cured? OMIGOD! Just by writing that down, I think I may have jinxed any chance I have of a full recovery! I take it back!!! Erase Erase Erase...

Sometimes Stargazer's messages creep me out. She said to "forgive" this past week. To "listen with my heart." My initial reaction was, Right! Forget it! Why should I forgive any of those jerks? But now, without meaning to, I think I've done that. It's such a relief to be chatting with those guys again. And yeah, I guess I have forgiven them. Now I don't remember why I took the whole science project so seriously anyway. It is just one report. One in about 7 billion a person does over 12 grades of school. And Shari and 2good didn't fake the data to be mean — they were just going along with the game. And like Stargazer says, we are all in this together — the 4 of us are each connected through school and through the way we've chosen to do school. We all have crappy stuff to deal with. None of us is happy with what is happening in our lives. We have so much in common, even though it doesn't seem that way at first.

How does she know to write all this stuff?????

Maybe I can try to enjoy what time I have left. No matter how it happens, or when, eventually I'm going to be dead, and I'll be dead long enough. No point being dead while I'm still alive.

Even More Recording and Analyzing

Forecast For the Week of
March 12 – March 18
by B.A. Stargazer

♊

Gemini (May 22 – June 21)

Wisdom arrives after a long hard struggle. You will need both twins to sort through the many messages that enter your conscious world.

From: cosmicgirl
To: jselenski
Subject: Research Project

Dear Mr. Selenski,

I tried tackling my science project again, but I don't know where to start. I went back to the Scientific Method outline and realize that I did successfully (I think) complete the first 4 steps of the "seven steps to discovery." Where things get messy is in the last 3 steps.

5. Record and Analyze Data
6. State a Conclusion
7. Share Your Discoveries

I recorded the data, but I can't analyze it because—as I told you—lots of it is false. Therefore I can't state a conclusion or share my discoveries either. (Unless you want me to share how angry I was at my subjects!)

Anyway, I'm thinking that if I did a good enough job of the first 4 steps, perhaps you could just mark me on that portion, and we'll leave it at that. Seeing as I did more than half the steps, I figure I should at least get a passing grade.

Does this sound fair and reasonable to you?

And by the way, I think I know FOR SURE what your sun sign is. You are definitely a Libra, who is known for being diplomatic, easygoing and charming. And because you're all these things, I know you'll give me that pass.

Yours in science (and diplomacy),

Kaleigh Wyse.

From: jselenski
To: cosmicgirl
Subject: Re: Research Project

Kaleigh,

Your last message brought a big smile to my face. I do indeed possess all those attributes that you listed. I'm not, however, a Libra. Guess again.

And I'm afraid I'm not going to let you off the hook. I would like a written report on astrology, on what it is and how it works.

Then I would like a report on why your data became unreliable.

I hope to hear from you soon.

Mr. J. Selenski

From: cosmicgirl
To: starlight
Cc: blondeshavemorefun; 2good4u
Subject: another request

Me again,

Stubborn Mr. Selenski is making me complete my report on astrology. I told him some of the data I collected was … fictional (to put it nicely), but now he wants me to analyze WHY that happened. What a pain.

Anyway, I hope you can hang in there just a little longer and consider the following questions.

1.   Did you read the daily horoscopes for Leo?
2.   If the answer to #1 is No, please explain why.
3.   If the answer is Yes, how did you find the experience?
4.   Did the horoscopes say anything that caused you to doubt their reliability?
5.   Do you believe the horoscopes held some truth for you the majority of the time?
6.   Did reading your horoscope change the way you behaved?
7.   Overall, do you think the horoscopes written by B.A. Stargazer are accurate
      – most of the time,
      – some of the time,
      – rarely?
8.   After being my guinea pig in this experiment, are you more skeptical about astrology, less skeptical, about the same?

Thanks!

Kaleigh

P.S. I may have to submit your responses to Mr. S., so please continue to write in school-type english.

From: starlight
To: cosmicgirl
Subject: Re: another request

Hi Kaleigh,

This is beginning to feel like work now! It was fun reading horoscopes, but all those questions!!!

Okay, here goes:

1.   Yes, I did read the daily horoscopes for Leo. And the weekly, monthly and yearly, but I guess you don't want to know about that.

2.   Yay! I don't have to answer this one.

3.   I found the experience fun. Reading the horoscope tweaked my imagination (as you know!). If she said that something "good" was going to happen, I felt hopeful all day and kept looking for it to happen. I basically felt up, even if the "thing" didn't come true. (She didn't use the word good—she was more specific—but you know what I mean.)

If the horoscope didn't sound too optimistic, I usually didn't think about it much, although sometimes it made me approach my day more cautiously.

I was disappointed when we no longer had to collect data. That could partly be because I enjoyed our emails back and forth. (And I enjoyed having a boyfriend. Lol) But I think it was mostly because she put a positive spin on most of her predictions.

4.   The horoscopes didn't say anything to cause me to doubt their reliability because I don't believe one astrologer can really know what is going to happen to every Leo every day. Sort of like weathermen. Their forecasts aren't always accurate either, but they usually are. If I didn't have a "hit," I assumed it was just an off day. I trust astrologers know what they're doing. Some are better than others. Some are way too vague. I really like B.A. Stargazer. (Do you think that's her real name? Lol)

5.   Yeah, I'd say the horoscopes held some truth for me most of the time. Of course, the way she writes them, they're often just practical advice that would do anyone good to read. For example, today for Leo she says, "Although you may have agreed to do something in the past, that does not mean you have to keep on doing it." That could be good advice for anyone. Hey wait! Does she mean us Leos don't need to help you with the rest of this project? Hmmm. :)

6.   Yep, reading my horoscope did cause me to change the way I behaved. I behaved badly. I became a liar. But I can't blame the horoscopes for that. I think the horoscopes would have caused

me to lead a better life (aside from the lying) because her advice was usually so positive and encouraged you to do the right thing.

7.   Overall, I think the horoscopes are accurate most of the time (see #4 above).

8.   I never was skeptical about astrology. I think the stars and planets do have an effect on our lives, but until your science project I never spent much time thinking about it.

I hope that helps.

Shari

P.S. Are you ever going to tell me about yourself?

From: cosmicgirl
To: starlight
Subject: Re: another request

Yep. Soon. :)

k.

Thanks for answering all those questions!

From: 2good4u
To: cosmicgirl
Subject: Re: another request

Give it up, Kaleigh.

From: cosmicgirl
To: 2good4u
Subject: Re: another request

I can't give it up! I've decided to finish this report. I've come this far. Just tell me some more lies if you want. I'll never know.

Kaleigh

From: 2good4u
To: cosmicgirl
Subject: Re: another request

Kaleigh,

Astrology is a joke. Stargazer and every other shyster like her is getting rich because there is a sucker—like you—born every minute. Those planets and stars are trillions of miles away. They are not affecting your daily life. I can't believe you or anyone else buys into that crap.

I am not a Leo. I am not a Gemini. I am not a Pisces or Capricorn or any other sign. I am a young offender in a juvenile detention home. I am not here because my parents gave me up to a series of fucking foster homes or because the stars determined I should be here. I'm here because I stole cars, broke into houses and got kicked out of all the high schools in my community. End of story.

I joined your little game because I needed a distraction from the boredom of this place. You sounded so cute with all your yabber about horoscopes. So sweet and naïve, so different than the girls I know. I'm sorry to hear you're sick. You didn't figure I could read between the lines? I'm not here because I'm stupid.

I guess I can understand why you've turned to astrology. Being seriously ill probably makes you do strange stuff, but I still think you should chill out. You were fun for a while.

Lucas Seymour

From: cosmicgirl
To: 2good4u
Subject: Re: another request

Lucas, I bet you're the same astrological sign as Mr. Selenski.

Kaleigh

From: 2good4u
To: cosmicgirl
Subject: Re: another request

Good one, Kaleigh! You're lightening up. Could this mean you're getting well?
And for a teacher, I always thought Selenski was cool. So thanks.

Lucas

From: cosmicgirl
To: 2good4u
Subject: Re: another request

I hope I'm getting well. I'm trying. And Mr. S. is pretty cool. I wish I could figure out once and for all what his astrological sign is!

Speaking of astrology, you're entitled to your beliefs, Lucas. I just wish I'd known what they were before I started my project. That way I could have done my experiment properly. The results would have been a lot more interesting.

By the way, you're right about me turning to astrology after I found out I had cancer. I'm sure that sounds pathetic to you. Maybe it is. I also lost faith in astrology somewhere along the way—about the time I discovered that the chemotherapy hadn't wiped out the tumor.

But now I'm beginning to find faith in it again. How would you explain that, Mr. Knowitall?

Kaleigh

From: 2good4u
To: cosmicgirl
Subject: Re: another request

Hmm. Could be you've found a hot new astrologer?

From: cosmicgirl
To: 2good4u
Subject: Re: another request

Very funny.

So when do you get out of that juvenile detention home?

k.

From: 2good4u
To: cosmicgirl
Subject: Re: another request

The answer to that is written in the stars.

(Could you please consult your astrologist for me and get the date? Thanks.)

Lucas

From: blondeshavemorefun
To: cosmicgirl
Subject: Re: another request

Hi Kaleigh,
Happy to comply with your request!! :)

1. Yes.
2. N/A
3. Enlightening.
4. No. Just the opposite. I doubted their reliability before I began reading them. I became a follower of astrology.
5. Absolutely.
6. Yes. I think. Though I still don't know whether the chicken or the egg came first (see data collected weeks ago).
7. Most of the time.
8. Less skeptical.

Jamie

From: cosmicgirl
To: blondeshavemorefun
Subject: Re: another request

Thanks, Jamie.

Have you heard from that girl from your Jedi chatroom? Is she doing ok?

k.

From: blondeshavemorefun
To: cosmicgirl
Subject: Re: another request

Yeah, she writes to me every day. I'm like her savior or something. It's a bit embarrassing the way she carries on. Now she wants to swap pictures. Ha. That should bring a quick end to her obsession with me.

I turned her into a horoscope junky too. Lol. In a strange way, it gives her something to believe in. I guess we all need that in our lives.

And hey! I still want to know who your imaginary friends are.

Jamie

From: cosmicgirl
To: blondeshavemorefun
Subject: Re: another request

Hey! I'm jealous. You're mine! Tell her to go find her own guy. LOL.

I was tempted to suggest you send her a picture of some hot rock star or something, but then I came to my senses. There's way too much dishonesty happening in chatrooms already. And besides, you should give the girl some credit. She'll probably love your face just the way you are. So don't send her anything! :)

k.

Oh, my imaginary friends were:
1.   an immortal twin
2.   an astrologer who doesn't respond

Don't you wish you had friends like these?

From: blondeshavemorefun
To: cosmicgirl
Subject: Re: another request

It does wonders for a guy's ego to be fought over. :)

There may be a lot of people establishing online relationships, and lots of imaginary friends, but they're sure limited, aren't they? I'd love to go to a movie, on a walk, or do something, ANYTHING! with you. Chatting just doesn't cut it.

Pouting,

Jamie

From: cosmicgirl
To: blondeshavemorefun
Subject: Re: another request

You're right. I'd like to do something with you, too. Maybe some-day, when we're finished school, we can plan to meet somewhere. Wouldn't that be fun?

Hey, listen to me planning for the future! I haven't done that for a while. Thanks, Jamie!!

k.

March 18

OMIGOD!!!

I'm practically bald, I may still have cancer, but Jamie wants to go out with me! Would that have happened if we'd sat next to each other in a classroom? He doesn't even know me. Or does he? I have no idea. I think I know him. For one very stupid moment I even thought I was falling in LOVE!! with him. Just what I told Shari she could never do online. Omigod.

I think I know Shari and Lucas, but what would it be like to be with them? Would they seem completely different? Would hearing them talk put a whole new slant on what they say? Would seeing them—no matter how open-minded I'd try to be—change the way I'd feel about them? Would their mannerisms, their voices, their ... I don't know ... their beings be something I liked? Or do I just like reading what they have to say? Will I ever find the answers to these questions?

Where is all the wisdom that was supposed to arrive this week?!

Stargazer said I'd need both twins to sort it all out. True, all those questions, no answers.

But at least I HAVE questions, which means I care about something. Not caring is the pits. Been there, done that. Hope not to do it again.

State a Conclusion

Forecast For the Week of
March 19 – March 25
by B.A. Stargazer

♊

Gemini (May 22 – June 21)

Take heart, Gemini. Great news
will arrive by July 1st. You are
the catalyst among friends.

From: cosmicgirl
To: jselenski
Subject: Research Project: Conclusion
Attachments: 1. Astrology Report 2. Leo Data

Dear Mr. Selenski,

As you can see, I've attached a written report on astrology that covers what astrology is, how it works, some historical information, etc. I hope you find it's okay, even though it's kind of boring. I have also attached my file of data, which I collected from my Leo subjects. Have fun wading through that mess!

What is not included in that report are some of my personal observations and conclusions about astrology, which I came to after attempting to do this project. I will discuss those here, in a sort of essay, if that's okay with you.

First of all, I want you to know that even though I have had some doubts about astrology over the past year, I'm now a firm believer again. Knowing you, Mr. Selenski, you would want me to PROVE to you that it exists, right? But I would ask you, can anyone prove that God exists? How about Love? Lots of people believe in God and Love, right? But no one can prove they exist. You can't see them, touch them, smell or taste them, but people would tell you that they FEEL them in their lives. And I'm sure you wouldn't dare argue with that logic. Well, I FEEL the presence of a cosmic energy in my life. I really do. Hey! Maybe the energy affecting the cosmos IS God! Anyway, we know that it's the gravitational force of the moon and the sun on the oceans that creates tides. If the sun and moon can move the oceans around, don't you think they could have an effect on human behavior? I think so. And I think that the other celestial bodies also have an effect.

What I have "discovered" about astrology (and I know how much you like that word) is that astrologers can't predict exactly what is going to happen in a person's life. They can only advise you of the kinds of energy that you can expect from the cosmos. We can choose whether to take that advice to help us create healthy and happy lives. For example, a common planetary force that astrologers warn us of is the Mercury Retrograde. I used to be scared of this scenario. I thought it meant bad things were going to happen to everyone. Now I know it only means that there are potential difficulties with communication. This just means that we should use extra care with what we say and what we interpret when chatting with or writing to friends (or teachers!).

Another thing I have discovered about astrology is what a powerful positive influence it can have on a person's life. Two of my Leo subjects were not horoscope readers before I began my project, but thanks to me :) they are now, and the horoscopes helped them make some good decisions. For example, one of the subjects was encouraged by her horoscope to confront a situation that was bothering her. So she did, and with very positive results! The other may even have saved a girl's life as a result of reading his horoscope. Now, I know you like to argue that horoscopes are vague and will be interpreted differently by everyone who reads them, but I ask you, Mr. Selenski, what's wrong with that?! Each of us can take the advice found in horoscopes and apply it to our own lives. I have discovered that the power of suggestion is very strong, and, I would argue, very powerful. LOL

The one thing about horoscopes that worries me a little is that some astrologers may not be as responsible and trustworthy as others. I don't think a responsible astrologer would ever say that something specifically "bad" was going to happen. They would only say that the cosmic energies didn't favor you at that time (or something like that) and you should take certain precautions. That seems fair to me. When I was going through a rough time with my radiation therapy, we Geminis were told by B.A. Stargazer that we'd be experiencing a solar low. At first I was appalled and even more depressed by this news, but the advice that followed was for us to take things slowly and to save our energy. I realize, in hindsight, that that was excellent advice, and I am glad that I chose to follow it! I guess there will be irresponsible astrologers, just as there are irresponsible doctors, lawyers, and even teachers. :)

In conclusion (and I know how you like conclusions, Mr. Selenski), I think I can sum up what I learned in the conducting of this experiment with the following quote from B.A. Stargazer.

"We are all influenced by the astrological climate—but it is just that—a climate. We each have the power to create our own lives. The stars help us to see realities and possibilities, but in the end, our destiny is what we make of it."

And here endeth my essay.

Sincerely,

Kaleigh Wyse

P.S. My horoscope for this week says I will receive great news by July 1. Now how can I NOT believe that?!

P.P.S. Are you an Aries? Energetic, quick-tempered, extroverted and sometimes aggressive?

From: jselenski
To: cosmicgirl
Subject: Re: Research Project: Conclusion

Dear Kaleigh,

I received your science project and your essay. Do you realize that you actually turned it in a week early? I think this is marvelous considering all you have been through this term. You earned extra marks for your promptness.

Now, your report on astrology is interesting. It answered many of the questions I had. I didn't find it boring at all. I also think you argued your points in your essay very well. In an earlier conversation, you and I discussed the value of trying to think positively. You have convinced me that the power of suggestion is very strong, and if astrologers can influence people to make positive choices in their lives, more power to them!

Just one question: where can I find these horoscopes by B.A. Stargazer? (LOL — to steal an expression from you!)

I am not an Aries, as I am very patient, which I think we determined some time ago. We must be almost through all the sun signs, aren't we?

Mr. J. Selenski

P.S. Did I mention I'm awarding you an 89% for your project? Congratulations.

From: cosmicgirl
To: jselenski
Subject: Re: Research Project: Conclusion

Thank you very much!!! (for the 89%) I hope the fact that I have (had????) cancer didn't have any bearing on your decision.

You know, I used to hate science. I thought it was a stupid subject. Lately, though, I realized that without science there'd have been no drugs to help me fight the cancer. Therefore, SCIENCE ROCKS!

Okay, I'm down to 3 sun signs—Pisces, Sagittarius and Capricorn. Which one are you?!

Kaleigh

From: jselenski
To: cosmicgirl
Subject: Re: Research Project: Conclusion

I'll give you a hint. I was born the same day as my hero, Albert Einstein. How's that for serendipitous?

Mr. J. Selenski

From: cosmicgirl
To: jselenski
Subject: Re: Research Project: Conclusion

Aha! You're a Pisces. Supersensitive, sympathetic, compassionate, and reclusive. So true. (And is it because you're reclusive that you chose to be a distant learner teacher rather than a classroom teacher?)

Kaleigh

From: jselenski
To: cosmicgirl
Subject: Re: Research Project: Conclusion

Kaleigh, no more questions!! (But my, you are inquisitive! Is that a Gemini trait?)

Enjoy your spring break, and I look forward to being your supersensitive, compassionate science teacher in the fourth term, when we will be studying metaphysics, one of my favorite topics. You may wish to get ahead on your reading, just for fun.

Mr. J. Selenski

Share Your Discoveries

Forecast For the Week of
March 26 – April 1
by B.A. Stargazer

♊

Gemini (May 22 – June 21)

The past is not an indicator
of what lies ahead. Dream. Be
creative. Sing!

From: cosmicgirl
To: starlight
Cc: blondeshavemorefun; 2good4u
Subject: We're done!

Hi Leo subjects and one other,

Phew! It's done. The astrology report has been written, turned in and marked. I received an 89%. Not bad for a completely messed-up project!

I wrote an essay for Mr. S. telling him what I discovered about horoscopes and astrology over the past 12 weeks. It was mainly about my belief that the cosmos does influence us in many ways, from our character traits to the kinds of energies that are going to affect our day-to-day lives.

What I didn't tell him was the other stuff I learned on this project, the stuff about role-playing, fantasies (a much better word than lies!), and hiding behind our computers. I have a feeling that these lessons will stay with me way longer than the ones on astrology. We've had our good times and our bad, haven't we, but I really want to thank each of you—even you, Lucas!—for hanging in there for me. You all submitted data—in your own way—and I learned a lot from it, even from the stuff that was make-believe (another great word). I know you all had your reasons for doing what you did, and I want to thank you all for spending "time" with me on this. The truth is, I'm going to miss working on this project. I've grown to like you all—a lot! I've spent a lot of time mulling over whether or not you can really get to know other people online, and I think I've come to a conclusion. I believe (for now, anyway) that a person may be able to conceal certain truths about themselves, but their true nature still comes across in their words, even if they think they're hiding it. I feel like I know each of you, and now, without this project, I'm afraid we'll lose contact. I guess we'll continue being distantstudybuddies for as long as we continue being correspondence students, but it sounds like we're all planning to be back in "real" school (even you, Lucas?) soon. But even if we do stay in touch, it won't be the same without swapping day-to-day stories. I guess what I'm trying to say is, I hope to stay close to each of you.

Thanks again.

Sending hugs!
Kaleigh

From: cosmicgirl
To: starlight
Subject: ps

Hi Shari,

You have been so right about me not sharing anything with you. I just wasn't ready until now. I really want 2 b good friends with you, so I'm ready to tell you anything you want. You ask the question, I'll give you the answer. I'll let you decide for yourself which answers are fantasy and which are true! LOL

Your friend,
Kaleigh

From: starlight
To: cosmicgirl
Subject: Re: ps

Kaleigh, you're a brat! LOL. But I love you anyway. I also know you're funny, friendly, caring, wise and lots of other stuff. Oh yeah, and a Gemini. What else does a friend really need 2 know?

Your bud,

Shari

From: blondeshavemorefun
To: cosmicgirl
Subject: Re: We're done!

Nice letter, Kaleigh, but I want to be MORE than friends. How does a guy do that online?

Jamie

From: cosmicgirl
To: blondeshavemorefun
Subject: Re: We're done!

Hmm. A guy could try phoning the girl in question. (540) 457-9324.

k.

But first I'd better do some checks. Are you a neat freak or a slob? Punctual or late? Is your belly button an inie or an outie? When you eat corn on the cob, do you chew around the cob or up and down the length? And most important of all—and this could really make or break things, Jamie... when you eat your smarties, do you eat the red ones last? :)

From: blondeshavemorefun
To: cosmicgirl
Subject: Re: We're done!

I believe I have the right to refuse to answer those questions on the grounds that my answers may incriminate me!!
j.

P.S. but yes about the smarties. :)

From: cosmicgirl
To: 2good4u
Subject: one more thing...

I meant what I said, Lucas. You may be the worst juvenile delinquent on the planet, but you've got a wicked sense of humor and an intriguing fantasy life. Will you stay in touch? And are you going to change your wayward ways once you're set free? Maybe go back to school? You are so good at "creating" yourself online. Why don't you "write" a new you—for real?

k.

From: 2good4u
To: cosmicgirl
Subject: Re: one more thing...

Not a chance.

2good

but I have a real good friend here who's looking for a hot e-pal.
Know any available chicks?

From: cosmicgirl
To: 2good4u
Subject: Re: one more thing...

Yep, but she only writes to hunky actors.

k.

From: 2good4u
To: cosmicgirl
Subject: Re: one more thing...

A perfect match.

TTFN

2good

From: cosmicgirl
To: B.A. Stargazer
Subject: I'm Back!

I bet you thought you'd never hear from me again! Lol. My last letter to you must have been a bit depressing. Sorry about that. I was going through a hard time—as you know. I felt like I was trying to make my way through a thick, murky fog. I could not see the light. Not even a glimmer. Well, that fog has lifted and I'm back, but just this last time. I thought you might be interested in hearing what became of me.

First of all, as you can see, I'm still alive! :)

When you didn't reply to my e-letters, I have to admit I was disappointed and a little hurt. You list your address on your webpage, so I assumed you wanted to hear from your fans. Now I realize you have been corresponding with me, just in a different way than I was corresponding with you. Through your Sun Signs column you've been giving me great advice, and warnings, but most of all you've given me hope when no one else could.

I've decided I may not become an astrologer myself (way too complicated figuring out those star charts), but I do know I will always be open to the messages that the universe is sending my way. Thank you for helping me see the possibilities.

Your loyal Gemini friend,

Kaleigh Wyse

March 30

Dear Immortal Twin,

I've decided to stay mortal for a while longer. I bet you were beginning to think we'd be swapping places in the very near future, didn't you! So sorry, but you'll have to wait a little longer. I don't know how long, but it won't be today and hopefully not tomorrow. With any luck it won't be for another 100 years, give or take a few.

Thanks for being there when I needed you. :) You never supplied me with any answers, but you sure were a good listener!

I'm going to stop writing to you for now. Oh stop pouting! :) I'll always feel your presence (that IS what I'm feeling, isn't it?), but for now it would be best for me to write or, even better, to TALK to real people. I never wanted to share my feelings about my cancer with my friends and family, cuz I thought I was burdening them. Because of that, my friends stopped coming to see me. They thought I was shutting them out. They didn't understand that I was trying to protect them. That almost happened with my distantstudybuddies, and I tried to shut out my parents, too. Mom and Dad never gave up on me, but it must have been hard for them. Now I understand that the people who love me want to listen to my feelings. People do want to help, and in the future, I will ask for it. Maybe. Lol.

Anyway, I felt way better about everything once I told my distantstudybuddies about being sick. It really unburdened me in a way I never thought possible. And I'm going to contact my old friends, tell them how I felt, and ask them to forgive me. Wish me luck!

I've been thinking of some of the things I can do now that the chemo and radiation are finished and I feel energized. There are things that I'd never considered doing before I got sick, and things that I put off doing til later. Now I know it's stupid to wait, and there are so many things I can learn. Where to begin??

I guess I'll start by going back to school. And then I'm going to join the choir and sing as loudly as they'll let me. Who cares that I'm tone deaf!

Not me.

Love always,
Your mortal twin

A teacher for a number of years, and now a parent, **Shelley Hrdlitschka** is a reader, writer and vocal proponent of juvenile and teen fiction. Shelley lives in North Vancouver with her family, and presents extensively to children at area schools. Her first book, *Beans on Toast*, a juvenile novel set at summer camp, was soon followed by *Disconnected*, a suspense/adventure novel set in Vancouver. *Disconnected* was a nominee for the South Carolina Junior Book Award and also for the Surrey Book of the Year and was very well-received by teachers, librarians, booksellers and, of course, young readers. The sequel, *Tangled Web,* was published in 2000.

Dancing Naked, the story of a girl dealing with a surprise pregnancy, is an International Reading Association YA Choice, an OLA White Pine winner, an ALA Best Book nominee and was on the ALA Quick Picks for Reluctant Readers list. It is also on the ALA's Popular Paperbacks list and continues to be a teen favorite.

Kat's Fall, released in 2004, is an ALA Quick Pick and an OLA White Pine nominee.

With three daughters, Shelley and her husband try to create "gender balance" in their home by sharing it with male animals— a dog, two cats and a guinea pig of indeterminate sex. Shelley is a member of various writing organizations including CANSCAIP, CWILL and the Children's Literature Roundtable. She is an avid reader with an abiding interest in juvenile and teen fiction. Shelley's astrological sign is Cancer, on the cusp of Leo, which she says makes her a crabby lion.

Shelley is available for media interviews, bookstore events, and school and library presentations.

Praise for books by Shelley Hrdlitschka

Kat's Fall

1-55143-312-5
$9.95 CDN • $7.95 U.S.

Darcy's mother is getting out of jail. Ten years ago she was convicted of throwing his baby sister off a fifth floor balcony. Kat survived, but Darcy has spent the last decade raising his sister, giving her the love and support she has been denied by an absent mother and an uncaring father.

As he grudgingly re-establishes ties with the mother he thinks he hates, he is accused of a horrific act. It will take incredible strength—his own and others —to fight the charges, but he finds that truth is often an elusive concept and that trust and love are powerful allies.

"…in this riveting story, Darcy is such a well-drawn character that the reader feels his pain…" —*VOYA*

"…this powerful novel is both heart-wrenching and shocking…" —*School Library Journal*

New York Public Library Books for the Teen Age 2005 List

Dancing Naked

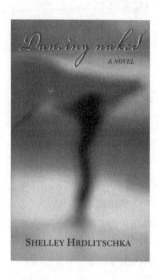

1-55143-210-2

$8.95 CDN • $6.95 U.S.

Kia is sixteen and pregnant. Faced
with the most difficult decision of
her life, she learns that the path to
adulthood is a twisting labyrinth
where every turn produces a new
array of choices, and where the
journey is often undertaken alone.

"…a heart-wrenching story…"
—*School Library Journal*

CLA YA Honor Book 2002

ALA Best Books Nominee 2003

ALA Quick Picks for Young Adult Readers 2003

ALA Popular Paperbacks 2003

White Pine Award 2003

IRA YA Choices 2004

Other books by
Shelley Hrdlitschka

Tangled Web
Disconnected
Beans on Toast